Reflections
A Love Story
part one

Dennis Waller

"Love doesn't know distance, neither in hours or miles, nor in life or death"

DEDICATION

CONTENTS

ACKNOWLEDGMENTS

Oleg Medvedkov, Charity Parkerson, Yvonne Crowe, Janis Hutchinson,
A special thanks to Natasha Andriese

and to Ernest Hemingway

"There is nothing to writing. All you do is sit down at a typewriter and bleed." -Ernest Hemingway

i

The Funeral

Texas 2010

It was a bright, sunny spring day on the 19th of April, Daniel's 42nd birthday. A picture perfect day, the world in full bloom with flowers in their glory, songbirds readying their nests, and a light breeze blowing through the new growth of leaves in oak and pecan trees. The setting resembled something out of a Norman Rockwell painting...everything the eye could see was filled with the glory of rebirth and renewed hope.

But Daniel saw none of it. He was driving to his wife's funeral.

He hadn't slept in days and left for church just as dawn broke. The sky was that special hue one could see only when the first rays of daylight began to break through the night. It turned alive with colors so vibrant and majestic, that the event seemed to be a reflection of Heaven's splendor. Yet this moment, so precious that words could not accurately describe it, wasn't enough to fill the gaping hole in his heart. Without his wife, without Vanna, all that was left was him...alone ...steering his car into the sunrise like a robot. He was on autopilot, doing what needed to be done, his senses numb. But there was more at stake than just going through the motions of attending the funeral, hard as that would be. Somehow there had to be a way he could still connect with her. If he couldn't find it, his life was over. There was no way he intended to live without her.

Daniel arrived at the church before anyone else and took a seat on the end of the front row. Soon after, friends and family began to filter in by ones and twos and milled around, gathering in small groups, lost in small talk in a vain attempt to break the nervousness and tension. All the while, no one wanted to approach Daniel. It was too awkward of a situation, one that everyone avoided. After all, what could they say? Daniel didn't mind. He appreciated being left alone with his thoughts.

She was only 29, too young and beautiful to be cheated out of life. The recipient of an assassin's bullet. The true culprit behind this heinous offence? Daniel had his suspicions.

Vanna was a friend, a sister, a daughter, and a wife. To Daniel, she was his life. She had completed him, the refinement and elegance that was missing in him. She rounded him out, and with her he was a whole person lacking in nothing.

During the funeral service, in the same church where Vanna and Daniel had been married just a few months ago, friends took their turn going to the front of the sanctuary to share their special memories of Vanna. Laughter and tears abounded as friends and family recalled their favorite moments.

It was Laura's turn to speak. She was Vanna's older sister, ahead by a single year, and Daniel couldn't bear to watch her make her way to the front of the sanctuary. To look at her was painful for she looked just like Vanna with her raven black hair, big brown eyes, and the sculpted cheekbones under alabaster skin. She was wearing dark blue jeans that hugged her curves and a butter-yellow cashmere sweater, a perfect foil to her dark hair and eyes, reminding him starkly of Vanna's shapely figure. Not only did she look like Vanna, she moved in that same easy style that always brought to mind a model on runway in a fashion show. It was more than he wanted to see. With his head down, he listened to her story and thought about how the family had agreed to keep the dress casual. Vanna would have wanted it that way and it didn't bother him. What you wore didn't matter, but what was in your heart...well, that was what always mattered to her.

Then it was Daniel's turn to speak. He slowly walked up to the podium, feeling as if he had aged ten years in the past few days. There was a rugged edge to Daniel, with his faded blue jeans, the brown Cole-Hahn loafers that Vanna had bought him for his birthday, and pale blue denim shirt that she loved to see him in. He cleared his throat and took a few moments to compose himself. Then without saying a word, he stepped down from the podium and walked over to the casket, pulled up a chair and sat facing her.

Placing his hand on hers, he took a deep breath, hesitated and began to speak. "I should have known better than to let you go. I should have made you stay. Now here I am all alone. What am I going to do?

3

Was it all just a dream? God knows how much I love you." He paused and then continued "But I'm mad at you...angry...that you left me here. I need you, I *need* you here by my side, but you're gone. You left me here! Alone! Yes, hell yes! I *am* mad, mad as hell because you did this...you did this to me." He raked his hand through his hair, his breath a harsh exhalation, and said gently, "I thought we were going to grow old together. I *thought* we'd find ourselves sitting on a porch somewhere laughing about the incredible life we had. I *thought* we'd watch our grandkids play in the yard one day. Hell, we haven't even unpacked all the dishes or finished painting the bedroom. I'm broken and lost. I don't know what I am going to do without you."

With a sigh he continued, "Even though I am mad at you for leaving me, I still love you so much." A small smile curved his lips, "Did you have any idea how happy your smile, your touch, and your kiss made me? Did you know that *every* time I looked at you I felt so lucky to have you in my life?"

Daniel got up from the chair and walked around the casket running his hand across the cold blue steel and stopped at Vanna's face, gently touching her smooth brow and brushing her dark hair back with his fingers. "We had so much life and love," he said, "so much to do, so many dreams to live, and now they are all shattered."

He bent down and kissed her, whispering in her ear, "Baby, I need you. God, *please*, just please... tell me what to do." With his head on her breast, he began to cry softly...the silk of her black dress soft against his face, the smell of her hair penetrating his numbed senses. In that moment, he knew that these final memories of Vanna would have to last the rest of his life.

Vanna's brother Bobby got up and moved towards Daniel in consolation but Daniel stood and motioned Bobby to sit back down. He took the white lace surrounding Vanna and placed it inside the casket smoothing away the wrinkles and tucking the lace around her as if tucking in child for bed. He adjusted the silver charm bracelet on her left wrist, placed a sprig of ivy and acacia with its small yellow flowers in her hands, flipped the hinge that anchored the lid of the casket open and slowly brought the top down. Standing stoic at the sight of her face, beautiful as it had ever been in life but now being surrendered to darkness forever, he said his last words, "I can't live without you. Promise me, Sweetheart, you'll be dancing in my dreams tonight."

Quietly, slowly, Daniel turned with his head held high and tried to smile among the silent tears as he walked to his seat and sat down. The Pastor, a small, bird-like man concluded the service, instructing that there will be a graveside service for the family, thanking everyone for showing their love and support of Vanna.

The ushers solemnly took the casket down the aisle to the entrance of the church. The only sound heard was the steady rolling of wheels across the cold marble floor. Daniel continued to sit there lost in thought while looking up at the cross of Jesus, undisturbed by those around him. Surely everyone knew his thoughts…"How could a loving God be so cruel?"

When everyone was outside and the family loaded into the black limousine, Bobby went back in, tapped Daniel on the shoulder and gave him a look that it was time to go. Without a word, Daniel stood and walked with him towards the limo. Bobby entered the limo first, moving over to leave room for Daniel and turned back to watch him get in but to his surprise, Daniel hesitated at the door.

"What is it?" asked Bobby in confusion.

"I'll drive my truck to the cemetery," Daniel said.

"I can ride with you," Bobby offered, eager to be a support.

"Thanks, Bobby, but I just want to be alone right now. I'll follow you there."

Bobby hesitated and Daniel thought that he would protest, but then he sighed and nodded, understanding Daniel's request for solitude. Watching the powder blue casket being placed into the back of the hearse brought a profound sense of dread. Daniel simply wanted to be left alone.

Starting up the truck, that one song, their song was playing on the radio. In an instant, Daniel was whisked away to happier times, but was brought back to a sober reality by the sight of the black Cadillac carrying his wife to her final resting place.

Pulling into the cemetery, he parked the truck to the side of the gravel road and sat there for a few moments as dust filtered into the cab of the truck. Looking for a way out, an escape to avoid this moment, Daniel sat in silence. He noticed a bottle of water on the floorboard that Vanna had left in the truck on that fateful day. He reached down, slowly removed the top, closed his eyes and drank. He wished he could hear her laugh, the way she always laughed when he drank from her water bottle and said, "You're going to get my germs." Placing the bottle back into the cup holder, he watched as the service started, desperately wanting to cry from all the hurt inside, but he couldn't.

Daniel never knew that love could hurt like this. Just the mere thought of being alone for the rest of his life after experiencing the fullness of Vanna's love was terrifying. With all his soul and heart, he wanted her back. He cried out her name and slammed his hands on the steering wheel in anguish, wanting to do something, anything to bring her back. He felt impotent, knowing that he could do nothing to change what had happened. Drowning in despair, he wanted to run, just get out of there and not face the yawning emptiness that awaited him. But cool reason prevailed. He got out of the truck and deliberately made his way to the service, still reeling from a reality he had never contemplated having to face. Shuffling forward, he hoped against hope that this was nothing more than a bad dream and that at any moment he would awake and she would be there smiling gently at him.

By the time Daniel got to the graveside, the Pastor was concluding the final prayer. Oblivious to the events going on, he walked up to the casket and pulled out a Sharpie. Leaning over, he started writing on the top. The Pastor, surprised by Daniel's action, didn't move to stop him but continued the prayer. The more Daniel wrote, the more-uneasy the family grew at what he was doing. They darted looks of concern at each other.

Daniel finished and sat down in the chair that was saved for him in the front row-a place he never dreamed he would be seated. He heard the mumbling of words spoken as if they came from a distance, but they couldn't penetrate the fog surrounding him. His head felt muzzy, wrapped in wool, insulating him from the cold reality while his body flushed hot and then cold. He could only stare at the casket in disbelief while Vanna and Daniel's family watched in helplessness, knowing he was in a state of shock and there was little they could do to help him.

As the family paid their last respects and walked by the casket a final time, the words that Daniel wrote on the casket became visible.

I know there's a reason, there must be a rhyme. We are meant to be together and we will survive this. We will stroll hand-in-hand again. When I said to you, "It's forever!" you understood that you would always be in my heart, always on my mind. And when it became too much, you would be with me. No one can replace you, only you can love me this way. Find your way back to me. I'll be here...waiting for you in my dreams...still crazy in love with you. Daniel'

Long after everyone had gone and only the workers remained filling the grave, Daniel sat defeated, staring at the ground. Each shovel of soil thrown on top of the casket separated him even more from Vanna.

In the last rays of daylight, as dusk began to fall, there stood behind Daniel in the sheltering canopy of a majestic oak the silhouette of a young woman wearing a black silk dress, her dark hair blowing in the evening breeze, desperately wanting to reach out to him in comfort and reassurance. She wanted to tell him that it would be alright and that soon...*soon* they would be together again strolling hand-in-hand.

Driving home, the sun setting, his thoughts drifted back to that warm September day, the day when the best thing that had ever happened to him occurred-Vanna walked through that door and into his life.

The Interview

Colorado 2055

Robert Wallen glanced at the calendar sitting on his nightstand upon waking. Today's date was circled, the 19th of September. This was an important day. Not only because of the *Rolling Stone Magazine* interview, but this was the day he had waited on for over 40 years. It held more significance than anyone could imagine. This was a day of reckoning. A day to settle accounts and close out the books.

Ian, his grandson and attorney, had set up the interview for him. Generally, there was nothing remarkable about granting an interview except that he hadn't given an interview in nigh on 40 years. Even Ian showed concerned about this change of heart. Though he was a successful writer, Ian had always held journalists at bay for him. Ian looked at lawyers, police and journalists in the same light as his grandfather, even if he was a lawyer himself. In his grandfather's words, "Don't have any use for any of those bastards."

With quite resolve and determination, Robert got up from bed and went to the wardrobe and chose his favorite pair of faded out blue jeans and a worn white denim shirt. The fabric like the man, was made from a rugged cotton twill. In Robert's mind, the wear and tear on the cloths showed character of a live well lived, like the man who wore them.

With anything that Robert did, certain conditions had to apply, even more so with this particular interview. First and foremost, it was to be at his cabin in the high country just outside Colorado Springs. Secondly, when he decided it was over, it would be over, and that was that. Considering that he had sold over 40 million books and not given an interview in close to 40 years, he knew *Rolling Stone* would have crawled on their belly for this coup. The fact that seven of his books had become blockbuster movies only whetted their desire to meet the legend.

***

It was Ian who ran the empire, took the meetings, handled the contracts and had complete power to make all decisions. As far as the world was concerned, Ian *was* Robert Wallen.

Ian had a shameless boldness about him, almost to the point of being arrogant, a common trait among attorneys. His strength, though, was in his good looks and an uncanny ability to express himself eloquently, and he knew it.

Ian had learned to accept his grandfather's eccentric behavior, even to the point of answering to the name 'Mark' when he was around him. Robert often teased Ian as being his Mark to his Alan, referring to Alan Watts, one of Robert's most admired philosophers. Robert said the most important lesson he learned from Alan was to accept and embrace who and what you are, no matter what that may be. That there is an indescribable freedom in surrendering to your fate and meeting it head-on.

After Alan Watts death, his son, Mark took over his father's work and continued with publishing his works. In the end, Mark Watts published more books than his father had while alive. Ian considered it a compliment being compared to Mark Watts, not fully understanding since Robert was alive and well. He wrote it off to Robert being 85 years old and kind of crazy anyway.

Ian never knew how the brilliant manuscripts came about or where the ideas came from and *never* asked. That was one place you never went. He still vividly remembered the tongue-lashing he received right out of law school when he asked Robert about a certain story he'd written.

"Why don't you go out and ask the rose why in the hell it is a rose and while you're at it, ask it its purpose and, of all the places in the world, why it picked that spot to grow?" Robert barked. "Whatever answer it gives, will be the same for me!"

"But Grandpa, it isn't going to say anything, it's a rose."

"Exactly!"

Every time Ian thought about that incident, he laughed. He understood now what his grandfather meant. Wallace Stevens, a modernist poet, said it best, "A poem need not have meaning and like most things in nature it often doesn't."

Ian agreed to escort the *Rolling Stone* journalist, Vincent Hendricks was his name, up to the cabin since no one would ever find the place on their own and he really didn't care to accept the liability of someone getting lost. It was a remote location, the way not well marked.

As Ian drove along the Aspen lined road, keeping an eye on Vincent's car in the rearview mirror, his mind drifted back to when he graduated from law school. After the ceremony, his grandfather congratulated him, "I always knew you would be involved with the law. Just didn't know which side it would be on."

Ian understood his grandfather, whereas his father held an unhealthy antagonism towards Robert. Their values were different but not different enough to warrant the quarrelling his father and Robert were prone to when together.

Getting his mind back on the road, Ian thought about how Robert would shred Vincent apart. Smiling to himself, he knew Robert loathed Vincent's type. The frumpy, Ivy League elitist who thought they were better than everyone else.

Pulling off the main road onto the red graveled path that led up to the cabin, Ian took a moment to marvel at the kaleidoscope of colors that seemed to come alive within the trees. The illumination of glistening threads of sunlight that found their way through the fall foliage created something magical, something special that seemed to contain a gloriously divine secret. The scene reminded Ian of a setting out of a C.S. Lewis novel. Ian understood why Robert was drawn to this place. He searched for words to describe the feeling, and muttered to himself, "A labyrinth of dreams."

Catching himself, Ian slowed down to stop at the front of the cabin. He chuckled at the thought of ramming through the cabin as he got out of the car.

Vincent who had parked next to Ian was already out and readying himself for the "meeting." Ian motioned for Vincent to follow him up the stairs to the porch. Along the way, he reassured Vincent not to worry. Roberts bark was worse than his bite.

As they reached the top of the stairs, Robert came out to greet them. Ian made the usual "Robert, Vincent. Vincent, Robert" introduction followed by insignificant small talk about the drive up and the weather. Ian had a distain for trivial conversation that held no value but knew that it was customary and tolerated it.

Once the introductions were made, Ian offered to stay but Robert assured him they would be fine. Besides, if there were any problems, he still had his 12 gauge shotgun loaded and ready in hand. While that didn't sit too well with the guy from Rolling Stone, Ian couldn't help but laugh and left.

***

Vincent Hendricks had been with *Rolling Stone* for years, and being more familiar than most with the works of Robert Wallen had been handpicked for the assignment. Being a professional didn't alleviate his nervousness at meeting someone of Robert's caliber. No writer's private life has inspired as much interest and fascination since J.D. Salinger. Robert was a deeply private man and only added to the mystery. The mention of the shotgun, while meant in jest, didn't help put him at ease.

"Well, Vinny, are you going to just stand on the porch all day or are you going to come in and get started? Jesus Christ, you want me to write it for you too?"

Vincent smiled and felt a sense of relief at the display of dry humor and walked inside.

Robert motioned towards the walnut table. "Take a seat, Vinny."

Vincent considered correcting Robert about his name but decided to focus on the bigger picture. He was about to bag the interview of a lifetime and let it slide. This was a career-defining moment for him. What he didn't know was that Robert knew this too and had already detected Vincent's hint of cockiness.

Walking to the table, Vincent noticed that the cabin was rustic by nature but well-organized as if a woman were living there. The living room, dining room and kitchen were all combined into one great room, with a loft above for the bedroom which Vincent could see. The floors were done in antique heart-of-pine, reminding him of the old colonial homes in Connecticut where he'd grown up. The massive library off the living room wasn't a surprise. He'd learned to expect that from authors, with the exception that this one looked like it came straight out of the Victorian era -a place not subject to the changes of time.

A fire burning in the oversized fireplace with a massive pine mantle cast a gentle light over the room. "Damn," he thought, "this is nice. I could get used to this."

"Very spacious and cozy," Vincent commented as he sat at the table.

Robert turned on the gas stove. "Want some tea? he asked. "It's Earl Grey. You're going to be here awhile so you might as well get comfortable."

"Yes, Sir, that would be nice. Do you mind if I get my stuff ready?"

"Not at all," Robert replied, nodding his head. "Go for it. I have to heat the water."

"I've have made out a list of questions. Okay to get started?"

Robert busied himself with making the tea. "Sure. Shoot, Kid."

"Well, Sir, no offense, but there are a lot of people who don't even know you exist. Most people believe that all of your books have been ghost written."

Without turning around, Robert laughed, "You might be on to something there, hell, they might even be right."

"Why is it that you never go out in public? Why the need to be such a recluse? I mean, the literary world already compares you with J.D. Salinger."

"What do you mean?" He cut his eyes over to Vincent.

"Well sir, this is your first..."

"Hell, I know what you meant. I go out all the time. To the grocery store, the hardware store, even to the movies. It hasn't been that long ago since I was in Vegas for a few weeks. I enjoy the sound of the slot machines."

"Then, how come nobody has seen you?" Vincent countered.

"Maybe they weren't looking for me," Robert offered.

Vincent scratched his head, confused at this response. He paused to contemplate his meaning but shortly gave up and simply asked, "What do you mean?"

"I go out all the time, I mingle with people. Do you know how many nights I've spent at Poor Richard's Book Store on Tejon Street? Yeah, I'm out all the time. See, the deal is, they don't see me because I am invisible," Robert replied.

"Invisible? Come on," Vincent laughed. " I'm looking at you right now."

"Yes, because you want to. It's your *job*. But to the rest of the world I am just another old man, an old man in the corner of a room that blends in with the drapes. The one nobody ever gives a second thought about."

"I find that hard to believe," Vincent protested shaking his head "I have asked around town and no one even knew you lived here much less claimed to have seen you."

Vincent could tell that Robert was growing frustrated with this line of questioning by the way he narrowed his eyes. Realizing this, he decided to change the topic before Robert reached for the shotgun and permanently ended the interview. He reviewed his notes to see if he had enough material when Robert placed the tea tray on the table with the three cups, tea bags already soaking in the steaming water. It reminded Vincent of the setting in a book he had read years ago, "The Book of Tea" by Kakuzo Okakura. "Is this in some way a Zen tea ceremony?" Of course, he laughed to himself, with all the hardware lying around it was more of a Remington Zen ceremony. He couldn't decide   what direction this interview was headed.

The walnut table where he sat had to be as old as Robert. The top was scarred from years of use but also worn smooth with age. It had character, more than he would expect in a table. The only incongruent element was a corner where someone had carved the initials, "dva4ever" Judging from its wear, it must have been done years ago.

Vincent quickly returned to his list of questions and asked, "Looking back over your career, a career that has spanned 40 years, do you have any regrets? Is there anything you wished you would have done but didn't?"

Robert took the seat opposite Vincent and without a second thought responded, "I try to live in the moment, in the now, you know? See," he waved his hand with a flourish, I don't live day-by-day, but moment by moment. If you can be happy *right now*, then you'll always be happy because *in the now* is always. Besides, the ghost of my past mistakes finds it hard to live in the present. As far as my failures go, I needn't be reminded. I haven't forgotten them."

Vincent didn't know what to make of his answer. He took a slip of the hot tea, forgetting to remove the tea bag, trying to digest what Robert meant. Looking at Robert, he could see the expression on his face, it was like a child at Christmas, that excited anticipation of opening the gifts. Vincent wondered what was about to be revealed.

Robert began to talk. "Son, I have a story to tell that very few men have lived to tell, and even fewer would believe. This is one of those stories that is in-between 'once upon a time' and 'no shit, that really happened.' Now, the fact is, it doesn't really matter what you choose to believe or disbelieve. Your belief or disbelief has no bearing on the truth. Whatever you think ain't gonna change what happened."

Vincent was dunking his tea bag, trying to remember exactly how to do this without looking like a fool and yet still listen.

Robert continued. 'Ought to be easy, ought to be simple enough. Yeah, man meets woman and they fall in love. But this house is haunted...' "

"Springsteen! From Tunnel of Love, right?" Vincent exclaimed.

"Yes. Yes it is," Robert said with a slow smile, his face revealing that perhaps he thought Vincent wasn't a complete nitwit after all.

Vincent perked up, "Yeah, Bruce Springsteen. You know, he was a famous musician back at the turn of the century. Did you know that some schools actually teach his music as a folk philosophy...along with others like Bob Dylan? Kind of a reflection of the times."

"I'm impressed that you know about him, and recognize one of his songs...that's impressive, son."

Vincent leaned forward. "I've always been fascinated by the music of that era. That was one of the reasons I became such a fan of your work, how you use music and poetry in your stories. I like the way you use it to convey emotion. Even as a kid, I could relate to the characters in your books by the way you used music to define them."

"Really? Well, thank you, Vinny," Robert said, acting surprised and pleased that he could have impacted someone with his stories.

Vincent, realizing that he was acting like a fan, silently berated himself for losing focus and apologized.

"No need, Vinny. I'm happy to hear that someone actually read one of my books."

Noting his sense of dry humor again and wanting to get on Robert's good side -if one even existed-Vincent replied, "Yes, Sir, about your story?"

Robert hesitated before answering, searching for the right words, finally saying, "You got to learn to live with what you can't rise above."

With that, Robert got up from the table, his chair scraping across the heart-of-pine floor and walked to the fireplace, and added three more logs to the fire. Once he had them positioned correctly, he crossed the room and sat back down again. The only sound at that point was the crackling of the fire.

Vincent studied the bones of Robert's hands. They were prominent, indicative of a long life lived, slightly swollen at the joints, a sign of arthritis and unsurprising given his age, but they retained a youthfulness in the way he moved, as if there was a young man trapped inside the decaying remains of a once great man.

"Yeah, man meets woman and they fall in love but it ain't meant to be." Robert leaned in confidingly, "Life is rough like that, he said with a wink, "sometimes taking more than it gives. I bet you most people are with someone other than their first choice, living a lie, all the while thinking of someone else. Blessed are those who find the one that is meant for them. But it seems that the only place that happens is in fairytales. He shook his head. "Maybe that's what makes it so sad. The more things change, the more they remain the same."

Robert paused and began stirring his tea, the clinking of his spoon against the cup and the crackling of the fire the only sounds. Vincent sensed something was about to be revealed, some untold secret. He waited, pregnant with anticipation.

"You have a wife?" Robert asked.

"No, Sir."

"Girlfriend?"

"Yes, we've been together for 3 years now."

"You trust her?" Robert asked, his grizzled eyebrow rising and fixing Vincent with a beady stare.

"Excuse me?" Vincent grew extremely uncomfortable. I should be asking the questions, Vincent thought, not him.

"Do you trust her?" Robert asked again, enunciating each word indicating the possibility that Vincent might be a nitwit and slow in understanding.

"Ah, yeah, I guess. I mean, yes. Why?" Vincent asked, bewildered. What exactly was this old man getting at?

"I find it funny, Robert continued, "how people will say they trust the one they love. But, how can you trust someone when you don't even trust yourself?"

Vincent shook his head. "I'm not following you."

"The next time you see her look into her eyes, and ask yourself...is it her that you see or some elaborate disguise? Her eyes won't lie," Robert explained.

Vincent sat there in silence, feeling uneasy and at a loss for words, thinking to himself, Damn! This guy doesn't waste any time. He's going straight for the jugular.

"You see, the two are connected...love and trust. The amount of trust you have is in direct relation to how much you love someone. It dictates how far you'd be willing to go for that person. A true love, a real love, is one where you operate in blind faith with complete trust. That's what is missing from most relationships. It is all about convenience nowadays. Most people live their entire lives never knowing real love."

Vincent was at a complete loss by now, thinking, what the hell is this guy talking about? They both sat there looking at one another. Robert had that look, a sly smirk, like a poker playing laying down a royal flush. Vincent welcomed the silence, giving him time to figure all of this out. Only the sound of the tree sap, being teased from the logs by the flames, popped in the uneasy void.

Robert broke the silence, "Have you ever heard about a love so strong that not even death could stop it?"

Vincent was stunned. "No, Sir, not really, except in the movies."

"What would you be willing to do for that kind of love?" Robert asked.

Vincent replied, "I don't know. I haven't really thought about it."

With his gaze on Vincent unwavering, Robert began."The tale begins with a guy, and just like a Bogart movie a woman walked right into his life. The moment he saw her, he knew she was the one..."

With his gaze still fixed on Vincent, Robert began, his face a curious mixture of tension and relief, as if he'd been waiting for this moment his whole life.

"The tale begins with a guy, and just like a Bogart movie a woman walked right into his life. The moment he saw her, he knew she was the one..."

If life is a tale to tell, I don't want a tragedy...I want a love story - part one

September 2008

It was a Saturday afternoon when she walked through the door and into his life. There was a street festival that weekend on the square, and his little curio shop was busier than usual. He enjoyed the brisk pace of the day as people wandered in and out of the store.

When she walked through the door he was struck by her natural beauty. Her black hair shimmered in the sun and she carried herself with the refinement of a Zhao Princess. Her brown eyes reminded him of cassia cinnamon, her skin glowed like a summer sunset, he thought like a man thinks when witnessing perfection in a woman.

She and her friend made small talk as they perused the items for sale, picking up this one and that one, making cheerful comments. It was obvious they were enjoying themselves, and they started collecting a few knickknacks to purchase.

Daniel could tell that she viewed his establishment as if she were walking through the door of a charming Ye Olde Shoppe, shelves overflowing with unusual and attention-grabbing objects. That pleased him. She was so fascinated by all of the interesting pieces that it was obvious that she didn't know quite where to begin. She looked like a small child in a candy store, looking at everything in wonderment. She unearthed a set of candleholders which were utterly exquisite in their simplicity. While she held them, she looked like she was drifting off to another time, to another place. She closed her eyes. What was she thinking or imagining? A couple having a romantic dinner by the light of candles softly burning in some stately home in an era long lost to history? The look on her face said she just had to have them.

Daniel maintained his professionalism in dealing with other customers, but that didn't stop his attention from wandering to her again and again. He tried to hide his stares as he continued catching glimpses of her out of his peripheral vision. "This woman is hot!" he thought. Simply—beautiful. When their eyes made contact, they shared an occasional smile. She seemed to enjoy the attention he was giving her, though her eyes would skitter away. She caught him eyeing her more than once, and continued returning his looks. Daniel felt good. Yes, they were flirting in an ageless dance, playing a little game of cat and mouse. It was time to make his move.

"Hi, I am Daniel, the curator and shopkeeper of this eccentric collection of treasures." He spoke in a mock Boston Brahmin accent. "How may I be of assistance?" This brought a smile to her face.

"Oh," she laughingly replied, "for moment I thought you were T.S. Eliot. Well sir, my name is Vanna. I wanted to get out and explore, to see what the town had to offer. I didn't expect to find such a place"

Staying in his Brahmin character, Daniel said, "If time and space, as sages say, are things which cannot be, the sun which feels. No decay no greater than we..."

Interrupting Daniel mid speech, Vanna said, "So why, Love, should we ever pray to live a century? A butterfly that lives a day has lived eternity."

Stunned, Daniel responded, "Very impressive, very impressive indeed!"

"You're not the only one, she said with playful confidence, who is familiar with the works of T.S Eliot."

They both fell into laughter at this impromptu exhibition of poetic recital.

Daniel was called away momentarily by another customer and saw Vanna turn immediately to her friend and whisper something. He kept one ear glued, but the noise of other customers prevented him from hearing what she was saying.

Occupied with a rush of customers, Daniel kept one eye on her. She and her friend continued shopping until most of the customers had died down, after which she worked her way to the counter to pay for trinkets she had found, giving them another opportunity to chat.

"I really love your store," she offered, as he wrapped up the ornate candleholders she had chosen.

"You'll have to come again," he said. "There is much to discover." His hand brushed against hers when handing her the bag of treasures she purchased.

He smiled at her, and in that moment time stood still for him. Somehow, he knew they had met before. Where and when, he didn't know, but the feel of her skin was something he seemed to know. His eyes knew the beauty of her smile, and the dulcet tone of her voice was a sound his heart remembered.

The rays of afternoon sunlight that beamed through the front window when she turned to walk away, created a silhouette of her figure, not only against the wall but in him. He felt the longing, painful lust as he stood frozen, hypnotized by an inexplicable feeling of knowing that they had loved before.

When the door opened, a light breeze tousled her hair. God, he had never been so pierced by a woman's beauty. How many lifetimes, he asked himself, have I loved you? How many times have you loved me? Just then she turned.

"Goodbye," she said with an enduring smile.

In that instant, he felt his heart glow with the memory of an unforgettable love. As easily as she walked into his life, she walked out, leaving him feeling even more alone than he had before she arrived. Maybe you can't miss something you never had, but this was one woman he was going to miss.

He walked over to the window and saw Vanna's friend taking a picture of her in front of the store. He sensed that he had just let the best thing that could ever happen to him walk out the door.

* * *

A few weeks later, on a slow Monday afternoon, she walked back into the store and into his life flashing him a big smile.

"Hi, Daniel, I'll bet you don't remember me."

"Hi, Vanna, you came back! He smiled, trying not to reveal too much of his excitement. "Yes, I remember you."

 "No way! You remember my name?   Wow, I'm impressed!"

"Oh yes, very well," he assured her. "It was a Saturday, the day of the Fall Festival. It was around 4:30 in the afternoon. You came in with a friend."

"Oh, that's just a lucky guess," she teased.

"You were wearing green leggings and a floral green and blue blouse, a charcoal colored shawl, and you had on a floppy straw hat. We also shared a T.S. Eliot moment."

She blinked with surprise and suddenly became speechless.   Daniel   flushed   slightly   with embarrassment and stood quietly, waiting for her to regain her composure while at the same time trying to recover his.

After what seemed like an eternity of awkward silence, she said, "I had my friend take a picture with my phone so I would remember where you are. This is only my second visit to town." She turned the phone around and held it up for him to see the picture.

There she was, just as he had described her, in front of the shop with a time stamp of 4:42 p.m. It confirmed what he already knew. He also knew what her first question was going to be and he had to make a decision quickly. Should he follow his heart and risk having her walk out of the shop thinking he was crazy? Or could he make something up like he had an eidetic memory? So distracted in trying to determine his next course of action that he was caught by surprise when she asked.

"How could you have remembered?"

He decided honesty was probably his best option and said, "I know this is going to sound like a pick up line, but the truth is…I found you unforgettable. You are so incredibly beautiful, there was no way I could avoid remembering."

He could see she was flattered but at the same time embarrassed. A small flush graced her high cheekbones and sheepishly cast her eyes down. He heard her emit a soft, "Thank you."

To cut the tension, he changed the subject, asking what her interests were. Vanna gratefully accepted the lifesaver he offered and began to talk.

They spent the rest of the day discovering each other in conversation until it was well past time to close the store. Daniel couldn't remember the last time he was so enthralled with talking to someone about such a variety of subjects. She was smart, well read, knew all about music, and they seemed to share so many common interests.

He learned that she was a student at the local university, studying for her Master's degree in

Finance. She had been born in Vietnam but decided to come here to Texas to keep an eye on her younger brother, Bobby, who was also going to school in the area. Even though she had graduated a few years earlier and hadn't originally considered pursuing a higher degree, here she was back in college. She had been a model briefly in Vietnam but had grown tired of the frenetic lifestyle and wanted a change.

Never had time flown so quickly. They both were surprised to realize how late the hour had grown, and she told him she couldn't remember the last time she'd had so much fun. He felt like the outside world had disappeared, until they both laughed and realized how late it was.

"I feel like I've known you forever," she laughed, "but it's late and I should go. Daniel felt a pang in his heart.

Do you need a ride a home?"

"Yes, thank you," she replied. Did he imagine it, or did she look like she was covering up that she was grateful for an excuse to spend more time with him?

As they were leaving, Daniel said, "I noticed that you were looking at that movie, *What Dreams May Come.* Why don't you take it home with you along with a few others? You can bring them back the next time you come in." It was one way he could guarantee he would see her again without seeming too forward.

"Really?" She smiled. "You don't mind?"

"I think you'll like it. It's about a love so strong that not even death could stop them from being together."

"Oh, I'm a sucker for anything romantic. Thank you so much. You're really very thoughtful. I'll look forward to watching it later tonight.

He drove her home. She lived across the street from the university campus in an apartment complex he was familiar with. Many of the university's students lived there or in the surrounding rental houses. She got out of the truck, leaned back in with a sweet smile and said, "Thank you, Daniel," her voice soft and delicate.

Daniel answered with a smile first, his heart thumping against his chest, and then answered. "My pleasure, Vanna. Anytime." With that, he pulled away from the curb.

Driving home, Daniel realized that never before had he been so fascinated and spellbound. His whole body filled with excitement, wonderment and bewilderment. What had come over him? He felt....*alive!* Even though he recognized that there is always nervousness   at   the   birth   of   a   new relationship, there was something different. Such a sense of peace and rightness. He wasn't falling in love; he was already *in* love.

For the first time in a long time he felt hope bubbling up inside of him like a fresh spring- dreams he thought long dead, now resurrected. Her smile was like a lighthouse that his heart had been searching for, a shining beacon along a treacherous coastline guiding his weary heart safe passage home. He knew that this was something special, this was destiny. But most of all, he remembered the promise he had made to himself, to find his one true love. He counted the minutes until she walked through the shop door again. And she did.

They began seeing each other almost daily, and. He felt complete in her presence. They were in perfect sync and they could get lost in conversation so easily. Dinners turned into marathons and once the owner of a restaurant had to ask them to leave since he had been closed for over an hour and wanted to go home. They laughed and left hand in hand. Daniel dreamed of the day when he would never have to say goodbye. The electricity between them made him feel so alive and so much in love.

Daniel knew their daily visits were rapidly coming to an end. She would be leaving to spend three weeks with her family in San Diego for the Christmas holiday. He wanted to make their last evening together special, and knew that the park had been transformed into a winter wonderland with Christmas lights and decorations. It was a bit chilly but not too cold for one last walk around the lake.

part two

Vanna couldn't stop thinking about Daniel, especially his eyes-a deep haunting blue, reminiscent of the blues in Monet's paintings that made it hard for her to look away. She had never seen eyes like his before. Every time she looked into them she felt a frisson of electricity and connection. His eyes pierced her defenses and she felt laid bare before him. She didn't know how to explain it but, in a magical sense, they seemed hauntingly familiar, like the ghost of yesteryears touching her soul, trying to get her to remember something that she lost along the way. She felt so comfortable talking to him. It was like finding a long lost friend that she hadn't seen in ages. After she left the store, after having Fran take a picture of her in front of the store, her thoughts were still of him. She found the way he walked sexy, a quietly confident swagger like he knew something she didn't.

The next day after he loaned her the movie and drove her home, again, he was all she could think about. She couldn't concentrate on her studies, she couldn't focus on anything.

As soon as classes were out, she grabbed the first bus downtown and breathlessly reached the door to his shop, her hand trembling on the handle. She took a moment to compose herself, smoothing her hair. What was happening? Was this real or a fantasy? Mentally shrugging, she took a deep breath and opened the door. And just as she hoped, Daniel's face lit up and he flashed her an immense smile. It felt like coming home.

They spent the afternoon in the shop talking about everything under the sun. And once again the afternoon passed into evening and it was time for him to close. He tentatively asked her to have dinner with him before going home and she eagerly accepted. Stumbling over her thoughts, she wondered if she were in love. Wow! Did she really just say that? Was it love? She wasn't sure but whatever it was, she wanted more.

She loved the way he looked, with his broad shoulders, waist tapering into strong, muscular legs and tight buttocks. This wasn't this first time she had noticed his body, and she felt hyper aware of the effect it was having on her. Tall and obviously in great shape by the way his t-shirt hugged his muscular frame and those jeans he was wearing showed the strength of his thighs, she felt as if she was in a heightened state of arousal and he hadn't even kissed her. She was on a whirlwind and loving every minute of it.

After dinner and a long evening grafting themselves into each other as one, he took her home to her apartment leaving her on the doorstep feeling euphoric, like a cloud floating on a breeze.

"Whew! What a hunk," She fanned herself. She didn't know what was happening or where it would lead, if anywhere, but she loved it and determined that she would to just go with it and not over analyze it, as she was wont to do. She wished now that she had kissed him before getting out of the car and mentally kicked herself. God only knew if she would have another opportunity.

It came with continued visits to the shop, walks in the park, late dinners and a continued sense of togetherness. The way he viewed life was so different to hers, she had never known anyone like him before. She hung on his every word as he talked about hearing what wasn't spoken, about seeing what wasn't visible.

"Reality," he explained, "isn't so much what we look at, rather it's what we choose to see. Everything is connected. There is no separation. Separation is only an illusion and within that illusion our view of the world is distorted, limiting the higher reality that exist just beyond our sight."

She felt...no, she *knew* she was falling in love.

* * *

She had kept her best friend Doan, back home in Vietnam, up to date with details of the budding relationship. They grew up together, living next door to one another. They were as close as sisters and shared all their secrets and had maintained that relationship throughout the years.

She emailed her every night before going to bed.

"I would describe Daniel as a hopeless romantic who idealizes the simple things. He breathes life into the most ordinary and they become extraordinary. He has such an elegant way of expressing his thoughts that it's helping me see life from a completely different perspective."

Yes, through Daniel's eyes, life was poetry in motion. A whole new world, a beautiful world was unfolding right in front of her. Night was no longer night. Even the strange and mystic light of the moon came alive. She felt the penetrating peace of its pale and gentle beams. And the stars? They now danced on a black velvet canvas in tempo with leaves rustled by an evening breeze with clouds floating by in parade.

"Doan, I've never experienced anything like this before. It feels like something from another time and place."

And when she received an email from Doan, then she remembered....

"Vanna, do you remember when we were both 16 and I dared you to visit an old Shaman that lived in a small village on the outskirts of town?"

Doan wanted her fortune and fate revealed but was afraid to go alone. Vanna, feeling challenged, reluctantly agreed though she didn't believe in it.

Until Doan mentioned it, she had completely forgotten. After all, it was just one thing among the multitude of silly things teenage girls do. They had been just kids really, with their heads in the clouds.

The village was nestled among the rice fields on a worn dirt road that was more of a path with the ruts of the wooden wagons that carried villagers to the rice fields every day. In the village of low-roofed wooden and tin buildings was a dry-goods store. Coils of rope and barbed wire, pots and pans hung from the eaves on the porch. Inside and out, there were hundreds of items on display- fish sauce and bean sauce, candles, and peanut candy. The store was so packed and dimly lit; it was difficult to distinguish one object from another. At the back of the store was a room where the Shaman held court.

The girls walked through the store hesitantly, not knowing what awaited them. Standing at the end of the counter was a small boy eating a bowl of rice. He stared intently at Vanna and Doan, his eyes riveted on the girls as they approached the opening into the room separated only by an ancient red and purple curtain suspended over the doorway.

On the other side sat the old woman at a table with a swarthy face, sunken eyes and leathery skin from years of being in the rice fields. She asked who wanted to go first. Doan eagerly volunteered. Vanna waited impatiently on the other side of the curtain, straining to hear what the old woman was telling Doan but was unable to decipher the muted voices.

When it was her turn, she entered the room. Lit only by light bleeding through the cracks in the walls, she sat down at the decrepit table on a stool. The old Shaman took her hand and told her an unbelievable tale.

"You will leave your home," she said, "and venture far away to another land. Once there, you will rediscover your soul mate, your "dom soul", the other half of a twin soul. But fate has a sense of humor," she warned. "This man will not only be older than you but of a different race."

Imagine being 16 years old and hearing something like that. Vanna grew disinterested as the old Shaman continued.

"There will be a moment when you will know this truth. It will happen when you look at this man with your heart, not your mind," she said tapping Vanna's forehead with one finger. "Within his eyes, you will know the truth."

That night, she and Doan had walked home sharing their fortunes, laughing all the way.

Now, so many years later, here she was at a destination foretold. Far from home - half way around the world - and now this man was in her life. Could he be the One? She had forgotten the Shaman's words until Doan mentioned the incident. She was having so much fun being with Daniel, she hadn't considered the past or the future. All that had mattered was the present. It was as if it had always been this way, she and Daniel together.

She stayed up all night, thinking about that night so long ago and far away. Back then, she'd had no desire to leave her country or date a man of a different race. But here she was, remembering what the Shaman had said. She was to know through his eyes.

She couldn't wait to see Daniel again, look into his eyes and see what was meant to be seen. Maybe the connection she felt when she looked into his eyes was the confirmation. Maybe *this* was the reason they captivated her. Thrilled at their continuing relationship, she would never forget their night of passion.

She knew she would only be able to see him one more time before she left for the holidays. She had family in San Diego and would be spending three weeks with them. She knew their next meeting would be important, one that might change her life forever.

part three

Daniel was nearly exploding with excitement. There was no way he could hold back any longer. This evening, he needed to tell her how he felt, how much he loved her and wanted only her. Daniel watched the clock and counted the minutes until closing time when Vanna called.

"I can't wait to see you, so I'm on my way there now. I should be there before you close for the night. I'll see you in a few minutes."

Her words were like a kick-start to his heart, making it pound like never before. He was more nervous about this night than he had been during that first meeting in the shop weeks ago. Business was slow so he decided to close early to give them more time.

When she walked in, he noticed something different about her.

"Can we sit down," she said, "and talk for a little while?"

"Sure," Daniel replied with raised eyebrows. "Is there something wrong? Are you okay?" He took her hand and they ambled over to a pair of wingback chairs and sat down. He raised one eyebrow inquiringly.

"Yes, everything is okay," she said. "I just have a story to tell you. It's about something that happened years ago back in Vietnam. I don't know where to begin. It is all so crazy, even I don't know what to make of it."

"What is it?" He leaned forward in his chair.

Vanna proceeded. She told the story about an old Shaman who told her how this day would come and the fate that was in store for her.

Listening attentively, Daniel thought to himself, "Could it be true? Were their souls locked together for an eternity as her story revealed?"

Although surprised to hear this tale, down deep he already knew the truth. Since his eyes first met hers he had known that they were two flames, twin souls that had reunited again. But he also knew that she would have to come to this realization on her own. His heart leapt with joy. She had.

When she finished speaking, they sat in silence holding hands, looking into each other's eyes. He noticed her staring deep into his eyes as if searching for something, her soul reaching out and touching his. He felt blissful, awash in a love that was beyond words, alive, like coming ashore after years at sea. The feeling that there was somebody for him and they finally found each other.

He felt their hearts beating in tandem. It was as if their souls had leapt together and were swimming in a pool of divine bliss.

"In ancient times," she explained, "it was believed that the soul was divided into two parts. Only when a person discovered their other half, would they become complete. It is the reunion of the "dom soul," the complete soul. Within that reunion, the one and only true and divine love can exist.

"I now know," she whispered, " what the Shaman meant. You are the One, my "dom soul"

Their eyes confirmed what their hearts already knew. They wanted to spend a thousand lifetimes together. They felt a warmth and radiance that was new yet familiar.

"I want to take you to the park one last time before you leave for the holidays." She nodded.

After parking, they walked among the brightly lit holiday displays along walkways that were surprisingly empty. The Christmas lights were twinkling and winking, lending a magical quality to the night's crisp stillness.

Along the edge of the lake the moon's reflection shimmered softly on the water, the effect mesmerizing. Each spoken word hung they shared crystallized in the air. They savored it, wanting to freeze it, never wanting it to end. Yet there was also an eagerness and intense desire to move forward and capture their destiny. With each breath Daniel took, he felt himself falling headlong, deeper and irrevocably in love. And he believed, for the first time, that she felt the same as he.

He sensed that she felt safe in his presence, sheltered and protected. He was a tall, strong man and his body radiated warmth like a furnace. As they walked, she snuggled closer, feeling the strength in his arm and chest.

"Even though we're alone in the park," she whispered, "I wish we were some place more … private."

Daniel felt an overwhelming desire to be close to her, to feel her skin against his. Waves of desire and need washed over them both. She was ready to become one in every way.

He stopped suddenly, turned and faced her. He spoke softly. "Her look reflected that she knew that what he was about to say was important. He had her full attention.

"Look at the moon," he said, his breath steaming in the cold air. "In a week, the moon will be full. And in San Diego, I want you to promise me that you will walk down to the beach on that night, take off your shoes and go to where the surf meets the sand." He looked down into her upturned face and continued.

"Still your mind so you may hear your heart. Raise your head to the moon and let the light shine over you while the surf caresses you, feel the water rush up and tickle your feet with grains of sand. And in that moment, I want you to close your eyes and listen for me. I will be there with you. I'll be the gentle breeze caressing your hair as it blows across your neck. I'll be the moonlight on your face, the sand dancing about your feet. I'll be there with you. Feel me and know you're not alone. It will be me caressing your body, loving your heart, mind and soul. Know that you are loved by me, and we'll always be together."

Then he held her in his arms, kissed her, and whispered, "I love you." And in her soft voice he heard, "I love you too."

After their walk, they went to their favorite restaurant for a late night candlelit dinner. They didn't talk much, they just spent the time being together, their spirits light, lost in each other's presence. The sound of her laughter, high and tinkling, was a symphony to Daniel.

After dinner, he drove her home. He walked her to the door, gave her a long, warm hug, telling her again that he loved her. With a lingering kiss, he left and walked toward his truck, unaware that inside she stood at the window watching him, whispering, "Bye, my love, bye." Then in a breath of frustration muttered, "Daniel, if only you weren't such a gentleman. Don't you know I want you to take me, love me, until I beg for release?"

Daniel sat in his truck and paused before inserting the key into the ignition. Then he leaped out and with a maddening rush dashed back to the door and up the stairs. She evidently saw him, for she flung open the door and jumped into his arms.

"I'm never going to let you go," she gasped. "Well, at least not until sunrise…"

Daniel covered her lips with his mouth. Their bodies became inseparable as they worked themselves inside her apartment and closed the door.

"Turn off the lights, baby." Their clothes fell to the floor piece by piece as they traversed the living room to the bedroom. "You're all mine tonight." Daniel whispered.

Her nakedness only heightened Daniel's excitement, his manhood standing and eager to claim her. He had fantasized about this moment from the first time he saw her. Stunningly beautiful, her breasts were high and perfect, nipples erect and dusky, inviting his kisses. He pulled her closer, hands cupping her ass, showering kisses on her lips, her neck, her breasts, leaving no part of her wanting. Her breath caught in her throat at the pleasure of having him, feeling his body flush against hers. A harsh moan escaped him as he continued his journey of discovery; God, she was so sweet! He felt like he was rushing but didn't want to stop for fear that he would wake up and this would be only a dream. She made soft mewling, pleading noises in her throat, unable to contain her pleasure. She couldn't wait any longer and took a step back, pulling him down to the bed. Spreading her legs, she cradled him with her body, reaching down to take his manhood and draw him into her wet, waiting body. She marveled at his hardness, like chiseled stone, an Adonis, her Adonis.

"Mine," he growled and began to move within her. "My woman."

They gave in to the passion that was riding them, their desire, their need to become one. Joined in an ancient dance as old as time, it couldn't have been more perfect. They passed the night in each other's arms, exploring, loving, until passion was spent and they drifted into slumber, only to wake and love again.

When morning came, they were tangled in a sea of blankets, and there was only the sound of their breathing as the first rays of the sun crept through the curtains. Where one began and the other ended, they weren't sure. But they knew that they were one, their hearts beating in tandem, both wanting this moment to last forever. While they felt a world apart, time raced, forcing them to leave their cocoon and venture out again. For her, there was a plane to catch and family to see. Time was running out.

* * *

A week later

Daniel began climbing the walls. He didn't realize how empty his days would be without her. How long could he take it? He had told her he would be waiting. The truth was that waiting was hard. Why must I miss her so, he asked himself.

Lying in bed, he listened to the rain beat against the window and the revolutions of the ceiling fan, but it was neither of those that kept him awake. No, it was the thought of being alone. He couldn't help wonder what was on her mind. These uncertainties cast a shadow over his thoughts as the clouds broke and a lone silver ray of moonlight shone through the window. The light cascaded across the room and he remembered what he had asked her to do on the night of the full moon. And there before his eyes was the full moon.

He didn't know how to explain it, but a sudden feeling of peace stole over him. He knew it sounded crazy, but it was as if the moon bore a reflection of her face. He went to the window and gazed at it, a smile lighting his face. Somehow, he knew she was at a beach in San Diego, looking at the same moon as he. He *felt* her...in his heart and soul. As the clouds returned to hide the moon's face, he released the curtains and returned to bed, filled with a quiet resolve and certainty. And he fell asleep, to dream of her.

In the dream, a song was playing in the background as he held her in his arms.

"Last night I slept, and saw you dancing in my dreams, just like the autumn leaves fall for you. All for you. You've changed my life, you've changed my ways. I don't even recognize myself these days. It must be a reflection of you. Only you.

I can't remember feeling love like this, I'm so alive. I can't imagine living life without you by my side. Day after day, you find a way to make this grown man cry. It's so true, I'm all for you.

My arms ache to hold you tight, keep you warm on the coldest night. My hand would brush back your hair from your eyes. For you. Only you. If I knew how to do it, I'd paint the moon and stars around you. Paint the perfect sunset. But I couldn't make it more beautiful than you. Oh, nothing…nothing compares to you.

Some might call it insanity. Without a doubt, for the rest of my life, I'm going to be crazy, baby, crazy for you. All for you. I'm all for you. It must be a reflection of you. Only you."

part four

Vanna settled back in her seat on the flight to San Diego, closed her eyes and let the smile she could deny no longer break free, imagining the rest of her life with him. How could she survive the next three weeks apart from him? She clung to his words. *"Promise me that you will go to the beach at full moon, close your eyes and listen for me. I will be there with you."*

On the night of the full moon, Vanna walked down to the beach. She took her sandals off and walked to the water's edge. It was there, as promised, that she stood with her feet in the sand and surf, lifted her head to the moon and marveled at the beauty of the night. The sky was clear and the stars shone brightly. The water came time and again to wash over her feet, the frolicking waves caressing as the sand danced playfully about her toes.

She stilled her mind, becoming more aware of the night breeze blowing in from the sea. It danced in her hair, its behavior playful and teasing. It seemed that the universe was alive and at play, her body the playground. A sense of love and peace came over her. She could hear the wind speaking, telling her that she would never be alone, that she would always by surrounded by love. On that beach, on that moonlit night, with the song of the warm breeze and gentle ebb and flow of the water, she was lost in eternity. She felt complete and whole as she experienced true love. On that beach, she found her love.

Beneath the same sky, though miles apart, she felt Daniel's presence. He was with her in spirit, in her soul, filling her heart with a love that she had never felt before. She had found the One, her "dom" soul. Her spirit gave birth to a song and she sang.

"If you'll come away with me, I will show you ecstasy, close your eyes and we will lead, and love will follow. Use your wings and fly away, and come with me today, your heart will lead the way, and love will follow."

part five

When Vanna returned from San Diego three weeks later it was with bad news. She had to relocate to Houston and would be leaving that coming weekend. Her brother, Bobby, was transferring to another school and she had to ensure that the transition would be smooth. He understood the concern she had for her youngest brother. Ever since the death of her older brother, with their parents still in Vietnam, she had accepted the responsibility of watching over Bobby like a mother.

The new development threw Daniel on a roller coaster. From reaching the heights of heaven, he'd plummeted to the depths of despair, rose again with joy at her return only to discover he was losing her...again. He was crushed, and yet he understood why she was leaving - it was a family thing. He respected it, respected her for her commitment to her family, but he refused to accept it.

Alone, Daniel desperately racked his brain for solutions. He considered selling his business and moving to Houston to be with her. He even contemplated asking her to marry him but couldn't ask her to choose between him and her family. Inside, he knew that this was something she was going to do and it was pointless in trying to talk her out of it. As much as he wanted to live the dream with her, he knew he would have to wait and see what the future held.

Vanna let him know that she was heartbroken over her decision. Part of her wanted to stay and be with him but she had to do this.

"My heart is begging me to stay, but it has to be Houston," she said. She tried her best to hide her anguish. He knew she didn't want the pain they both felt to diminish the joy they found in each other during these precious last days. They both knew the separation would be a serious test of their love.

Daniel helped with the move and they spent the weekend together in Houston, but the long drive back home did nothing but make him see again how empty his life was going to be without her. Maybe it was having nothing to stare at other than the vacant road stretching out ahead of him, but melancholy enveloped him and a dark shadow crept over his soul. The cold, sobering fact was that he was going home...alone.

They talked everyday by phone and exchanged countless emails but nothing could take the place of her touch, her smile, or her kiss. Weeks turned to months and April came quickly with its showers and renewal, awakening the earth from its winter slumber. Daniel's birthday was coming and fell in the middle of a week. He and Vanna had planned to do something special the next time they got together, but their conflicting schedules only created another obstacle.

Daniel resigned himself to spend his birthday as he had every other day, with no plans but to stay busy. It helped keep his mind occupied. Vanna had called early in the day to wish him a happy birthday and promised to make it up to him the next time she saw him. She asked him if he would go by the university later that day to pick up the gift she had sent in the care of a friend. Did he have time to meet her? Her friend would be free around six o'clock that evening and would text him with directions.

Daniel thought about how sweet and thoughtful Vanna was to arrange for him to receive a gift on his birthday. But that didn't diminish his desire to have her there with him. Soon distracted by the busyness of his work, time rushed by.

He forgot about meeting Vanna's friend until he received a text from an unknown number asking if he was going to be able to meet at the school at six o'clock. He texted back and agreed, asking where. Looking at the clock, he saw that it was already 5 minutes before six o'clock and if he was going to be on time, he had to hustle. Quickly locking the shop, he went to his truck and headed toward the university. On his way, he received another text asking his current location and estimated time of arrival. Not wanting to admit that he was running late, he asked instead where the friend was. She replied that she was waiting by the tower. By then, he was pulling into the parking lot.

Walking towards the tower, he didn't see anyone standing around and texted again, announcing his arrival. He was instructed to keep walking around the back side of the tower. He turned the corner and froze in his tracks, speechless with shock. He sucked in a quick breath of surprise. Standing there before him was Vanna, smiling and holding a birthday cake, her eyes full of tears. Never had he dreamed this would happen. At once, he knew that one way or another, Vanna would be his wife. Never again would he let her go.

Regaining his composure he ran to her and took her in his arms, weeping softly. No one had ever done something like this for him.

They sat at the base of the tower and fell into small talk while Vanna fed Daniel tiramisu cake from the box with a plastic fork, He could tell that she felt immensely satisfied with herself for having surprised him. It was the best night in a long time for Daniel. They spent the rest of the evening getting reacquainted, talking, kissing and finally, making love. With the warmth of her body next to him, Daniel drifted to sleep, knowing that somehow everything would be alright.

Morning came too soon and Vanna had to be back in Houston later that day. Daniel drove her back to the airport for her early flight. On the drive in, he vowed to himself that he and Vanna would be together regardless of obstacles.

At the ticket counter, Daniel decided this was it. As they walked to the security gate, he stopped and got down on one knee.

"Vanna, I can't live without you. My days are empty, my nights are torture. Will you marry me?"

Surprised, she gasped, her trembling hand covering her mouth. In a sob of relief she replied, "Yes" and threw herself into his arms to the sound of clapping and cheering from the people gathered around them.

Daniel didn't have a ring but that didn't deter him. With a flash of inspiration, he remembered the silver charm bracelet he had planned to drop off at the jewelers for cleaning later that day. He pulled it from in his pocket, fastened it around her wrist and embraced Vanna with a new found confidence.

"If feeding you cake was all it took to make you propose, she laughingly said, I would have brought you some cake a lot sooner." Holding each other, they both knew this was meant to be. Brushing her hair away from her cheeks, he kissed her and said, "I'll be waiting here for you, Mrs. Addison."

She smiled. "You had better be!". With that, she disappeared through the security gate. Even though it hurt to see her leave again, he knew this time he could endure it. He knew *now* they had a future.

The next weeks flew by quickly and soon Vanna was home with Daniel. Their first order of business was to find the perfect house and then get married. Vanna wanted her family to attend the wedding. It was a busy summer, with the shop to run, searching for a home, and planning a wedding. While there wasn't much free time, Vanna and Daniel had never been happier.

Interview- Continued

Vincent sat at the table in front of the crackling fire listening intently, waiting for Robert to get on with the interview. He was here for a story, and one way or another he was going to get it. There was no way he could go back to New York without something. He would be disgraced beyond measure if he blew this.

Robert had asked him if he ever heard about a love so strong that not even death could stop it. People always had love stories to tell, but he had a lot of questions to ask first. This interview would definitely make his career at *Rolling Stone*. He propped his chin on the heel of his hand and leaned forward intently. He'd listen to Robert's story first, and then get to his questions.

"We need a break," Robert said. "Besides I need to use the restroom. Getting old really sucks. There's things you miss, like taking a piss on your own terms."

Vincent, slightly disappointed, politely laughed and got up too. He would take the opportunity to stretch his legs and look around. An investigative journalist before joining *Rolling Stone*, he had been trained to look for things that other people easily overlooked.

Robert entered the bathroom and Vince glanced about the cabin. Strange, that after all of the awards Robert Wallen had amassed over his lifetime, there was no collection on display - not even a single family photo or the Oscar he won for his work on a screenplay. Man, this guy is really a recluse, completely cut off from the world. What is this guy hiding?

He stepped outside for some fresh air, a welcome change from the traces of smoke from the fireplace, and noticed no car in the driveway. There were remnants of an old truck covered up with a tarp on the side of the cabin, but it looked like it hadn't seen the pavement in years.

"How does he get around? Not that he should be allowed to drive," he grumbled under his breath, considering his age. He was finding more questions than answers when Robert called out to him from the front porch.

"Hey, getting hungry?"

"Sure, I'll have whatever you're having," Vincent made his way back up to the house.

Robert was constructing sandwiches at the kitchen counter when he entered, and placing a mixture of deli meats, cut vegetables and condiments on a plate. Vincent ungraciously hoped the old man had at least washed his hands before handling the bread. It seemed Robert read his mind.

"Yep, no need to worry. He chuckled. "They're as clean as cold water can get them."

Vincent, without responding, resumed his place at the table thinking this grandfather must have a sixth sense. He immediately focused on the list of questions he wanted to ask, forgetting momentarily about the love story.

"Robert, getting back to the questions. I have one, if you don't mind..."

"Yeah, I know, but let's get back to the story," Robert interrupted.

Argh. Vincent crimped his mouth realizing now that he had never had control of this interview. It had been an illusion orchestrated by Robert Wallen himself. So, with a display of half-hearted enthusiasm, he said, "Sure. So, what happened next after the proposal?"

"Well, Vinny, everything was going well for Daniel and Vanna. They found the perfect house, had the perfect wedding, even though they had to wait until February to marry. Her parents came from Vietnam as well as her sister who was living in Barcelona."

"Sounds liked a pretty big affair...the wedding, I mean."

"Not really." He made a casual movement with his hand. "They kept it simple. Even with the family, it was a small gathering. The date of the wedding didn't matter to Vanna or Daniel, they had each other and that was all that really mattered to them."

"So, is that the end of this little fairytale?" Vincent couldn't help but say it, hoping he could move on to his questions.

"Oh, no," Robert assured him, ignoring his sarcasm, "not by any means. In fact, it's just the beginning. A few months after the wedding they had a little spat, a 'lover's quarrel', and Vanna left and walked into town. Poor thing...she walked right into a police shoot-out. It was spring, as beautiful as ever and she was killed like a dog in the street. Daniel never forgave himself for that; he always felt responsible even after learning that it hadn't mattered what he would have done. It was fated to happen."

"A spat?" Vincent asked in disbelief, raising an inquiring eyebrow. "I thought this couple was beyond having a spat."

"Well now, it really wasn't a spat. Vanna had planned it, a diversion if you will, to get away from Daniel that morning. Why? She had something important she needed to do. It was supposed to be a surprise for him. Anyway, she was killed. They had a funeral, and the story continues....

Sweet Reunion

After the funeral, Daniel remained in a state of numbness. All he could think of was how to end this nightmare and turn the calendar back to a happier time. His desire, his wishes, all that he could ever hope to have was taken away from him. Death was the nemesis that had become his foe. Searching for a way around the law of physics, he found himself dwelling on how to create a miracle, one that would bring Vanna back. His fear was that he couldn't.

His second fear was madness ... or maybe not. At least in madness, it would be less disturbing, hoping that this orderly universe would somehow tolerate disorder and grant him his wish. At stake was his sanity. Yes, he was willing to bear any cost in his quest to be reunited with Vanna.

He had never known before the emptiness of waking up in the middle of the night alone after dreaming of Vanna. It was a feeling that was becoming his constant companion. Unable to sleep, he would sit in the library at night. It was the one room that had drawn them to the house. they converted it into a library, and It was the only room in the house to have been done in heart-of-pine, and that included the floors, the bookshelves, even the moldings around the door and windows. He told her how the heart-of-pine had to be older than the house itself, wood like that just didn't exist anymore.

That was one trait they both shared, a love for the old and rare. Vanna loved seeing Daniel's books lined up on the built-in bookshelves, along with his leather topped desk beneath which was a red, antique Persian rug. Enamored like a kid at Christmas over Daniel's excitement over the wood, he told her, jokingly, that if they ever sold the house he would take the room with him.

* * *

Vanna understood what Daniel shared with her about the wood late one night while watching medallions of candlelight dance through the room. The tightly woven grain of the wood seemed to come alive in shades of auburn and burnished gold. The beauty of it made her realize that there was so much to life, so much to experience - that there was a world hiding in plain sight just waiting to be discovered. The room, like something out of a Victorian mansion, had an air of refinement and elegance, reflecting two qualities in Daniel that she adored.

By accident, she discovered his writings and pressed him to let her read some of the stories but he had refused. She found it oxymoronic how Daniel could be such a strong and confident man, exhibiting decisiveness and resolve, but when it came to his writing he became fragile and insecure - a stark contradiction to the man he showed to the world.

She sneaked into the library at night before bed and read the short stories by candlelight. Captivated by the way Daniel wrote with such deep emotion, she would draw her knees to her chest and sit in his chair, lost in the romantic tales he wove, evoking in her wonderment and a desire for an era long gone by.

She could imagine Edgar Allen Poe sitting there at the same leather-topped desk writing, *Nevermore*. For her, the library became a portal to another time.

* * *

Daniel knew about Vanna's late night reading but he didn't mind. He could tell she had been reading by the way she passionately held him after coming to bed.

Maybe that's why he spent so many nights sitting in his chair, trying to imagine Vanna sitting there reading his stories. She even admitted that she became so engrossed in reading that she would lose track of time and be caught by surprise to see dawn breaking over the tops of the trees.

On the desk sat a photo of Vanna that he had taken at the park on their very first date, her long, dark hair braided over her shoulder. She wore a secret smile, her eyes lit with some private joke. Looking at the photo, it was obvious she had what it took to be a model. Even in a two dimensional photograph, her depth and radiance showed through.

Within the confines of their little library, with his memories of Vanna, he found some measure of peace, a small scrap of solace. That room held a connection between him and Vanna. At times, he swore he felt her presence in the quietude of early morning. And like Vanna, time seemed to slip away. Before Daniel realized he had been in there all night, the morning sun would paint the sky with streaks of pink, yellow and gold.

* * *

A few weeks later

On Vanna's last day alive, she bought some chrysanthemums for the flowerbeds that bordered the front porch. She bought them in silent riposte to Daniel's teasing her about planting all the ivy around the house. When they bought the home, there was nothing left but a few shrubs, with an elaborate lattice work around the house where there once were roses. At the sight of the lattice, Vanna knew that one day they would be covered in ivy.

"Ivy will attract fairies," she said.

Daniel didn't know if she was serious or just playing with him. But it didn't matter either way to him. He enjoyed the togetherness. He went as far as making an ornate sign proclaiming the house, "Ivy Manor," and placing it near the front gate. He even started to call her 'Ivy' in jest, saying it was a befitting nickname since they lived in a forest of ivy.

He knew Vanna didn't mind. She kind of liked it, even the little sign by the front gate. After all, she had started it by calling his old '64 GMC pickup truck 'Ginny'. She said that he and Ginny went together like peas and carrots, using her pitiful version of a Forest Gump voice. That always got a smile and chuckle out of him. She even went so far as to call him 'Lieutenant Dan' when she needed a hand, knowing he would ask her afterwards, "Is that all you got?" to which she would reply, "Can you handle what I got?" The playfulness of it all warmed her heart.

Secretly, Daniel was proud to see Vanna take such an interest in landscaping and helping him with the remodeling of the house. He thought it sexy for a woman to get her hands dirty working the soil and swinging a hammer. The sight of her standing on a ladder in her cut-off jean shorts and little leather tool belt drove him blind with lust. What's worse, she knew it. The house was fast becoming their home. Together, they were building a life, a beautiful life. But that was then and this was now.

The chrysanthemums were still sitting there by the front porch in their little black nursery pots. Daniel had been watering them but couldn't bring himself to plant them by the porch. He avoided them because of their constant reminder of Vanna's death. To have to walk by them each day as he left the house and returned again was more than he could bear. He felt that if he put off doing something about them, then he could put off actually dealing with her death too.

Daniel decided to plant the flowers at her gravesite instead. They were coming into full bloom and it seemed fitting that they be with her. Throwing some gardening tools into the back of the truck along with the flowers, he drove to the cemetery. The morning was becoming a warm, sunny day with a light easterly breeze. To anyone else, it would be a beautiful day, but these sunny days hurt the most, reminding him of the day she was buried.

Daniel picked out two lots on the edge of the cemetery. While walking the grounds looking for the perfect spot, he stopped under a majestic oak tree at the top of the hill, the highest point within the cemetery. Standing there in the quietness and solitude of the shade, watching the lush green grass sway in the breeze with nothing but blue sky for a backdrop, he knew this was the place for her. This section of the cemetery had just opened, and the absence of other headstones helped to create the feeling of being at a park. The name of this area was Serenity Point, befitting for someone like Vanna. He knew he had to choose wisely. This place was to become his second home, or so he thought.

Vanna's headstone was granite, engraved with her name and bordered by hearts and angels. He paid extra to have the stone made and installed as quickly as possible. He didn't want her to lie in an unmarked grave without some sort of acknowledgement. She deserved more than that.

While on his knees working the dark soil at the base of her headstone, he felt the intense longing and dread, missing the magic and love they had shared. He thought, Life isn't fair and wondered if God knew the hell he was in. Most of all, he wondered if he would ever see her again.

Drained and disillusioned, tamping down the soil around the freshly planted flowers, he heard a playful voice and his heart stopped.

"Why do you grieve for the living among the dead?"

Shaking his head, he mumbled, "Now my dreams are talking to me, I guess I must be going crazy."

Then he heard a laugh and the sound hit him like a lightning strike. He knew that laugh but he was hearing the impossible. Kneeling there frozen, immobile, he didn't know what to think or what to do.

"Stop being silly!" the voice chided.

With that, he turned around and there she was, standing under the sheltering arms of an old oak tree.

She was as beautiful as he had ever seen her, wearing the black silk dress she had been buried in, standing barefoot in the grass, brushing her hair back from her face to reveal a brilliant smile that was so familiar it squeezed his heart. He stood up in disbelief.

"Well?" she said with an insouciant grin.

With a voice that sounded detached and distanced, as if another person were speaking, Daniel said softly, "My God, it's you."

He felt a tsunami of emotion building deep inside, rising, filling every crevice of his being with a tidal wave of love and joy that was more than words could describe. His hands began to tremble. Tears of joy flooded his eyes and blurred his vision as the wave of emotion crested and fell - he didn't need his eyes to tell him what his heart already knew.

Dropping the hand shovel with abandon, he ran to her, took her into his arms and spun her around holding her tightly as he could, not believing that this was happening, or even *could* happen. In that moment, he didn't know if this was a dream or if he had died. The only thing he knew for certain was that he had Vanna back and that was enough. If this was dying, then he was grateful to Death for he held Heaven in his arms.

Kissing her lips, and feeling her warm, soft skin beneath his fingers, the saltiness of her tears in his mouth, the fragrant cloud of her hair, he knew she was alive. With Vanna in his arms, it was eternity in a moment, a lifetime of ecstasy at once. All that was lost was now found.

Swimming in a sea of amplified sensation, love overflowing, laughing and crying with joy, Daniel heard Vanna whisper softly in his ear.

"I love you, Darling, I love you so much. How I have missed you. I'll never leave you again."

Still shaking, he took Vanna by the hands and took a step back to marvel at her beauty. "It's always going to be you," he said, "that I love."

"Baby, I'm back," she said. "There was no way I was going to leave you, never in a million years."

"But how did this happen?" Daniel cupped her face with his soil stained hands.

Vanna shook her head "Not now, Daniel," she said. " Let's just enjoy it." Taking his hand, she said, "Take me home."

Walking hand-in-hand to the truck laughing together, Daniel couldn't imagine how life could be any better. He wasn't even sure his feet were touching the ground. If this was a dream, if he was crazy, he couldn't think of a better way to go nuts. He opened the squeaking driver's side door.

"When are you going to oil that door?" she laughingly asked.

Daniel chuckled and reached behind the front seat to grab the can of WD-40 and sprayed the hinges.

"Anything else, milady?" He gave her a wily smirk. Seeing her smile with those beautiful brown eyes, there wasn't anything else that Daniel wanted. He had it all. Waiting for her to get into the truck, he felt he was flying on the wings of an eagle, soaring high above the earth, free from the chains of grief that had ensnared him. Vanna reached over and grabbed his arm to pull him into the truck. She held on like she would never let go, and then leaned her head on his shoulder.

"Are you still mad at me?" she asked in her little sheepish voice, referring to the argument they had had before her death.

"Hell, no!" he blurted out. and started the truck, the tires kicking up dust and gravel behind them as they drove into the setting sun...headed home.

* * *

On the drive, Vanna was quiet. She had no idea what had happened to her. How could she answer the questions that were bound to come? It could only be by the grace of God that she was getting this second chance. She'd been at his side from the moment she had died, and the agony of watching Daniel the past few weeks since the funeral was more than she could bear. It was a hell that no one should have to endure. Standing there at the foot of their bed, night after night, watching him struggle to sleep, there with him while he sat in the library talking to her photo, wanting desperately to comfort him, was a pain she never wanted to experience again.

She prayed silently. Please, whatever has happened to bring us back together, let it last forever and never separate us again.

This was where she belonged, next to her man, her "dom" soul.

* * *

Coming home Vanna insisted that Daniel carry her over the threshold. He willingly obliged, sweeping her up into his strong arms and carrying her effortlessly into the house that once again became their home. Once over the threshold, he walked directly to their bedroom.

"Oh, really?" she teased. "But I've just come home."

"Off with these clothes and *then* off to bed," he ordered.

Giggling at the corny line, she began to unbutton his shirt as he carried her to the brass bed. He brushed his lips against hers and then traced a burning trail to her neck. Her breath came more quickly with each kiss until she turned her head and met his lips with hers. With the last remnants of their clothing removed, he laid her on the bed and joined her there, kissing, touching, igniting a fire in her that threatened to consume her until she begged him breathlessly to take her.

Raising himself over her, he probed her gently, stoking her flames ever higher. He ran his hands through her hair until he reached the back of her head, pulling her face to meet his, their mouths parting and tongues dancing in wordless agreement. She let out a soft murmur of contentment as his hardened manhood entered her, her tormented flesh quivering with pleasure at their union.

Daniel savored every minute, wanting it to last forever, not knowing if this was just a dream or if he would wake up. He felt her body quiver over and over as she found her release, reminding him of the first time they had made love. Their connection was still undeniably strong. He wanted their loving to go on and on, but his flesh, so long denied, soon joined her in that place, another dimension where there was no time or space, only now.

Content and sated, they held each other. She laid her head on his chest and ran her finger across the ridges of his ribs and abdominal muscles, tracing their taut outline.

"Remember that movie," she asked, "that you gave me when we first met?"

"You mean, *What Dreams May Come*?"

"Yeah, that's the one. Like the movie...as beautiful as heaven is, it isn't heaven without you. My place is here with you, in your arms. I love you."

Without saying a word, he turned on his side and gazed into her eyes. He prayed that whatever was happening, even if it meant he was going crazy, would never end.

"I love you too." He pulled her closer and they made love again slowly, lost in a world created just for them. It truly was a heaven on earth for them. A love so strong and profound that not even death could end it. They were no more separated by death than by life. It was as if they had transcended into another realm.

The Run

It was a beautiful spring morning and Vanna had gotten up earlier than Daniel. After a cup of coffee she decided to go for her morning run before Daniel and the rest of the town awoke. Dressed in her running gear, she headed out the door as she had done a thousand times before. It was like her feet were on auto-pilot as she ran, enjoying the breeze and crisp morning air.

In the middle of town she turned onto Main Street thinking she would take a short cut back home. She rounded the corner, her thoughts focused on her pace, respiration and the thrum of her heart, picturing her circulatory system doing its job, cleansing her organs, releasing toxins in each droplet of sweat, each exhalation of breath. *God it felt good to be alive!*

Just as she passed the coffee shop, she felt a sudden, intense pain in her abdomen. She winced and grabbed her stomach. Another jolt, like a lightning bolt brought her crashing to the ground.

Kneeling, gasping for air, she tried to draw a breath but couldn't get any air into her lungs. As the edges of her vision began to dim, one final blow hit her chest with the force of a freight train. Falling forward, she curled into a ball of pain, her brain frantically trying to make sense of it. Desperately trying to breathe, all she could see were pearls rolling in slow motion on the sidewalk. Confused and in immense pain, she looked up and saw a figure shrouded in darkness reaching down to take hold of her but she fought it. At that moment, all she could think of was Daniel.

This must be a dream, she convinced herself, nothing more than a dream. The pain faded and she pulled herself upright with the help of a nearby telephone pole, at the same time noticing her reflection in a store window. But she wasn't the only one. There, in the background stood a dark, ghostly figure. It spoke.

"You don't belong here. This isn't your realm any longer. You must return."

Scared, all she could do was turn and run home as fast as her feet could carry her back to safety, back to Daniel.

As soon as she hit the front door she went straight to the bedroom and jumped into bed where Daniel was still asleep, confused and sickened at the thought of what all of this might mean. Shaking uncontrollably and trying to catch her breath, she cuddled close.

Daniel, disturbed from his slumber, turned around and asked sleepily, "What's wrong?" But all she could say was, "Hold me, just hold me and never let me go."

He held her in his arms, trying his best to comfort her.

"Shhh....it's okay, it's okay. I'm never going to leave you, baby, never. I'm here, I'm here." Caressing her hair, he nuzzled up to her and held her tight, his lips against her ear.

"Nothing is going to stop us from being together. Not now, not ever."

* * *

Later that morning, while cleaning up the breakfast dishes, Daniel knew something was terribly wrong with Vanna. She was clearly shaken. He made two glasses of iced tea for them and encouraged her to talk about it but instead she deflected, wanting to know instead how *'it'* happened. 'It'… as if the horrific experience of her death could be contained in a word so small. She wanted to know, but deep down she was also afraid.

Daniel knew that Vanna was in denial, wanting to avoid the intrusion of reality, clinging to the miracle they were experiencing.

"You don't remember, do you?" Vanna just looked down and shook her head.

"Sit with me," Daniel said as he sat at the table. She joined him looking lost and confused. She began to shiver like a frightened child and looked up at Daniel, searching his face, "Please tell me."

Sitting across from each other at the table, clinging to each other's hands, Daniel took a deep breath and began, haltingly at first as he sorted through his own emotions.

"You wanted to go shopping for a wedding gift for Carissa when we got back from the nursery with the chrysanthemums. Remember, I didn't want you to go?

'Stay with me,' I asked you, 'while I finish painting the bedroom.'

Vanna let a smile come to her face and said, "Yeah, then you jokingly said, 'Yeah, I'd rather stay here with the weeds than look for a wedding gift."

Daniel replied, "I asked you to wait. I pleaded with you to do it later, to stay, but you were insistent on wanting to get it over with. All I wanted was for you to be here with me.

"Call it selfish, but I grew irritated. I felt you were being stubborn and hard headed. I couldn't understand why you were so hell bent on wanting to go right then and there by yourself and why you wouldn't wait. I offered to drive you but you said, 'No, I want to walk because the day is so beautiful.' I stood there by the back of the truck unloading the flowers and potting soil as you walked away." He paused and laughed..

"I stopped to watch you walk, and seeing your ass in those jeans I thought how could I ever be irritated with you? I love the way you look." I called out to you, 'I'll go with you later,' but you just waved to me and laughed while you wiggled your sassy butt.

You turned the corner and that was it…the last time I saw you alive. The rest is what I was told by the police. They said it happened fast, that there was no chance for anyone to react or get you out of the way in time. One cop said that you just walked right into it. You didn't have a chance," Daniel choked out, overcome by the emotions he had held at bay for so long.

Vanna tried to fight back the tears, but they streamed down her cheeks.

Daniel shifted in his chair, searching for a way to continue reliving that moment and convey it without losing his self-control. He reached out for his glass of iced tea and took a slow sip deliberately taking his time. Almost unconsciously, he pulled a plate of chocolate cake closer, reached for the knife balanced on the edge and began to carve initials on the corner of the table while contemplating how best to continue the story.

Vanna's expression let him know that she realized it was as hard on him to tell her the story as it was for her to hear it. She pulled his hand close to her and said, "Please?" Her eyebrows lifted in silent expectation.

"It was some crack-head," he continued, "that the police were chasing. When he got to the corner of Main Street, a cop pulled up and blocked him with his cruiser. He turned around and the police ordered him to stop and exit his vehicle with his hands raised. Every cop on the street had their guns drawn. They had him cold. There were two cops standing just outside the coffee shop right in front of him, maybe 50 feet away. They said that he just sat there, looking for another way out. The cops told him again, get out with your hand up and that was when he pulled out a gun and just started firing.

Daniel stopped again, his face crumpling as he broke down and said under his breath, "You know, it is all an illusion, thinking that you have everything under control. Only fools believe that and I was a fool. I never thought that something like that could happen. I know we are all going to die someday but not like that."

Vanna reached out, touched his chin and lifted his head, looking deep into his tortured eyes. "Please?"

Wiping his eyes, Daniel tried to smile and with a deep, shuddering breath found the courage to continue.

"They said that just as you exited the shop with your bubble tea in one hand and your package in the other, the crack-head fired three shots. You were standing in the line of fire when the first shot hit you in the abdomen, the second shot in the chest. When you fell to your knees, the third shot hit you in the heart. That's when the two cops had a clean shot and were able to return fire.

They said you were laying there in a fetal position with your head turned, looking up and that you died instantly. But I don't believe that because one witness said you reached out towards the telephone pole with your hand before taking your last breath. Needless to say, the crack-head died by the time the cops were done shooting. And all over $20 worth of useless crap he stole from some store up the street."

Leaning back in the chair, he stretched his legs under the table and momentarily placed his hands behind his head then back onto the table.

"Between the time of your death and the funeral, I was besieged by every attorney in town, showing up at all hours of the day and calling non-stop. A reporter had discovered a plot by the police department to cover up your death. Rather than the crack head's bullet shooting you, ballistics showed that the kill-shot was from one of the cops. It was never proven and some thought it only a rumor to sensationalize the story. Once that leaked out, I had every reporter in the world camped out on the front lawn. I couldn't take it anymore, none of it mattered anyway. What difference did it make? Regardless of who shot you, you were dead and would remain dead.

"The day before the funeral, I took the shotgun and went to the front porch. I fired a shot into the air to get everyone's attention. Then I shouted to them.

"'The next lawyer or reporter that speaks to me will be shot dead! I know all too well that I will go to prison for life, but rest assured you will be very dead.'

"When I fired the second shot a little lower, everyone cleared out, even the police that were there to keep order. The sad thing was, I wasn't bluffing. I have no use for any of those bastards." Daniel got up from the table.

"Stay here, I'll be back." He left the kitchen for a few moments. When he came back, he carried a shoebox. Sitting down he placed the box in the middle of the table and continued his story.

"The police called me to the station to pick up your personal effects. When I got back home, I sat down here right here at this table and went through them. I opened the package you bought to see what was so damned important that you couldn't wait for me to go with you. When I saw what you bought, I broke down and cried. It all made sense, your wanting me to stay behind. You didn't go to buy a wedding present for Carissa. You went to get me something for my birthday."

Opening the box, he removed with great care a pair of brown Cole-Hahn loafers.

"After you died, I held these shoes like I was holding you. God, the guilt I felt and the sense of loss, if ever there were a time when I could have taken my own life, it was then. I have only worn them once, and that was to your funeral. Next to you, these shoes mean more to me than life itself."

"That's the box from the library, isn't it?" Vanna tilted her head inquisitively. "The one with my photo on top?"

"Yeah."

"So, you basically created a memorial out of the shoes I gave you. Right?

"Yes, that's right."

Vanna sat in silence. She ran her finger lightly over the black lid, its embossed white lettering bringing back memories of that fateful day.

What happened in front of the coffee shop earlier that morning," she said, "now makes sense.

"I remember how I lay dying on the ground, gasping for breath and finally succumbing to that yawning darkness that beckoned me. And I remember my last regret-not being able to tell you one last time how much I love you and how precious you are to me. Then, everything faded to black.

But now that I remember, it's a kind of relief. But there's one question which remains a mystery. Here I am, sitting at the table with you very much alive, when by all rights I should be dead." She shook her head. "How?" She stared into space looking past Daniel to the kitchen window when she gave a sudden start.

"Daniel! Look!" She sputtered, pointing at the kitchen window.

"What?" He jumped up and turned to look.

"I can see the silhouetted shadow of someone reflected in the window standing behind me." She got out of her chair, wheeled about to check, and saw nothing. Then she froze.

"There it is again ... those words." She grasped Daniel's arm.

"What words? I don't hear anything."

She plopped back down in her chair, terror reflecting from her face. "They're the same words I heard yesterday, when I went into town." She shivered. '*You don't belong here. This isn't your realm anymore. You must return.*

"Daniel, what is going to happen?"

Daniel gaped in stunned silence as Vanna buried her face in folded arms on the table. Was there some power in force over which he had no control that would take Vanna away from him again? Frantic despair etched across his face. He couldn't lose her again. He lowered himself slowly back into his chair. Then, he remembered.

"Sweetheart, I think I know what's been happening."

Vanna raised her head, blinking away the tears.

"Weeks before I met you," he began, "I had a strange visit with a monk. We were debating life after death, and this is what he said.

'Spirits can manifest in this world three ways. One, by those of a pure heart, like a child, that still have ties with this realm. Two, those seeking the spirit unaware that they are not of this world. And lastly, by a love that transcends the realms.'

"Vanna, I know for sure that it was our love that brought us back together. But the monk also said there was an order in the realms and that a balance has to be maintained."

""Who is this monk?" Vanna asked, now at full attention.

Daniel felt a mounting dread in his core before answering her.

"First, before you came back to me, I kept thinking I saw a reflection of the monk in the windows and mirrors. I dismissed it, thinking that lack of sleep had brought on an illusion caused by my grief and exhaustion-."

"Well, who is he?" she interrupted, leaning forward intently. "Did he say any more?"

"That's what I'm getting at. In recalling his last words to me I now have suspicions of who he might be. He told me, *'The greatest con ever pulled by the devil is convincing the world he doesn't exist."*

"You mean," Vanna said, her eyes wide, "the monk be the devil himself? What does it all mean? What does it have to do with us?"

Daniel said, "No, I don't think the monk is the devil. But I still believe he is more than a monk. Maybe a messenger, a guardian? Who knows but the reflections I seen in the windows and mirrors the last few weeks weren't of the monk, it was somebody else."

Daniel shrugged his shoulders and made a helpless gesture.

"I don't know. I just don't know."

DENNIS WALLER

The Reckoning

It was September 19th and even though it had been a while since the incident, Vanna remained frightened and too fearful of stepping one foot outside of the house without Daniel at her side. He was her talisman of protection. She tried her best to put on a cheerful front, not wanting to worry him, especially considering his every-day admonition to her.

"You can't let that one incident stop you from enjoying life."

The interesting thing about his comment was that there were aspects of their new situation that neither one of them talked about. It was avoided and ignored, as if by sheer will they could make it of no effect. First, no one else could see Vanna except for Daniel. Second, she had been killed and buried but here she was, alive and well. Third, they both thought that they were crazy but didn't want whatever was happening to end.

Determined not to let her fears overrule her, Vanna mustered the courage to go on her morning run. She loved running at daybreak and missed the birth of a new day and all the opportunity inherent in it.

She got up, dressed as usual, and headed out the door. Very few people were out at that time of morning but it didn't matter, they couldn't see her anyway.

Running through town, she made a point not to go down Main Street, she didn't want to risk reliving her death again. Coming to a red light, she stopped and ran in place. While waiting for to change she noticed a man on the other side of the intersection. She could swear that he was looking right at her. But how could he see her? She shook her head and dismissed it. Of course he couldn't see her, no one but Daniel could. The light changed. She ran across the street and kept going, but as she passed the man, she came to an abrupt stop. He spoke to her.

"You don't belong here. I've been sent to take you back. Out of kindness, I'll give you 24 hours to get ready. But after that, you will be leaving with me."

Though terrified, she held her ground, "What do you mean? Who are you?"

With a sardonic laugh, he continued, "You are no longer of this existence - you *died*. Therefore, you must go back to the realm where you belong, the one you've moved on to. It is forbidden for spirits of your realm to interact with mortals. That's my job, to keep the balance and ensure that spirits like you stay where you belong." She started to speak but he cut her off.

"Look, save me the sob story, I've heard it a thousand times before. Whatever you have to say, it doesn't matter. This is the way it is and always has been. So, in 24 hours I'm coming. Be ready." With that, he left and continued down the street.

Fear shuddered through her like a cold wind. If she was terrified before, then this was a level way beyond anything she had ever experienced. She could almost hear a clock ticking away the seconds, counting down to the end of this second lease on her life. She did the only thing she could do, turn around and run back home to the safety and refuge of home and Daniel.

While she ran, she tried to make sense of it all and what was supposedly going to happen. How could she tell Daniel?

She rushed through the front door to the smell of bacon frying and fresh coffee brewing. She paused for a moment to collect herself, then went into the kitchen. Daniel stood at the stove lighthearted and happy.

"You timed it just right," he said giving her a smile. Give me just a couple of minutes and breakfast is served." The look on his face told Vanna that he was completely oblivious to the torment and fear whirling inside of her like a toxic cocktail.

Remaining in the doorway, she watched Daniel, her thoughts centering on how this was where she belonged. *This* is my realm. *This* is my heaven. At that moment, she made a decision. "This" was worth fighting for, and together they could overcome any obstacle, no matter how big. No matter how impossible it seemed, their love had power.

Over breakfast, she managed to tell Daniel in a matter-of-fact way the messages she had received from earlier reflections and about the strange man that morning. He listened intently while eating, as if news of a mysterious, dark messenger was not enough to get between him and his stomach. Without apparent concern or looking at her, he asked, "What did he look like?"

She put down her fork and stared at him. "You're going to think this is crazy but he looks like..."

Daniel interrupted, "Jet Li?"

"Yeah," she replied. "The Chinese film actor."

Her breath momentarily stalled in her throat and she replied in astonishment, "Yeah. "How did you know?"

Daniel continued eating, stopping to take a sip of coffee between bites, then after taking in a deep breath said, " I've seen him a time or two. He's been in the shop before and we've had a few talks. He said his name was Lin Xin. If I didn't know any better, I would swear he was Jet Li. When I first met him, I thought he was as loony as a toon, but once we started talking, I couldn't get over his depth of knowledge. If I had a dollar for every time we debated the meaning of Lao Tzu's works..."

Vanna puzzled over his nonchalant manner in responding. But, then again, he had always demonstrated a sense of calmness when things were falling apart.

"Daniel, tell me more about Lin Xin, she pressed.

"Well, he claims to be royalty going back to the Shang dynasty in the second millennium BC. But wait, it gets better. He said he lived in a city, Zhengzhou, the home of dragons and that his father was the emperor of the realm and he was a prince. He Lin Xin was also a corrupt politician He had a younger brother named

Ching Siu-tang, a righteous man, a man of the light, who was a white sorcerer, one who practices only white magic. For this, he was known throughout the lands as the Dragon. Now Ching had a daughter, Zhang, who inherited this white power and was thus known as the Snow Leopard."

"Lin Xin, even though he was in line to claim the throne, was envious of his brother and niece's powers. He was also angry that he could not corrupt them to help him take over the seven kingdoms and serve as the supreme lord ruler over the all the realms."

"Because of his greed and jealously, he killed his brother over a dispute. He knew that his niece, Snow Leopard, held the same powers, and that she would avenge her father's death by killing him. This would leave her as the sole heir to the throne. In a fit of blind rage and anger, he killed her too." Daniel leaned forward and propped his elbows on the table.

"The eternal sentence for his crimes? To walk the earth collecting lost souls. According to the legend, one of the souls he claimed was that of Lao Tzu. Lin Xin arranged to let Lao Tzu go free in exchange for the meaning of the Tao, thus allowing Lao Tzu to be a spirit that could travel between the different realms."

"For this transgression of bribing Lao Tzu and giving him that power, he was sent to the Shaolin Monastery in the Pagoda Forest. There, he met Nagarjuna who revealed Lin Xin's fate before his own untimely death of being beheaded.

It is said that the life span of Nagarjuna was attached to the King Udayibhadra. This king had a son,

Kumara Shaktiman and he wanted to be the king. The wife of the king and Kumara's mother, had instructed Kumara that in order to become king, he would need to cut Nagarjuna's head off. The mother also said that since Nagarjuna is such a compassionate man that surely he would agree.

Amazingly, Nagarjuna agreed. However Kumara couldn't cut off his head with a sword. Nagarjuna said that in a previous life he had killed an ant while cutting grass. Therefore, due to karma, only the blade of kusha grass could cut Nagarjuna. Kumara did this and was able to behead Nagarjuna. Strangely enough upon his supposed death, the blood coming from the severed head turned into milk and the head spoke, " Now, I will go to Sukhavati but I will enter this body once again." Upon this revelation from the talking head, Kumara separated the head from the body as far as possible. However, legend states that every year the head and body become closer and closer to each other. When the head joins with the body, it is said that Nagarjuna will return to this world to walk again.

Nagarjuna told him after his beheading, that Lin Xin would continue to live as a man but with the strength of the gods. *But," Daniel added with emphasis, "*only as long as Nagarjuna continued to reside in Sukhavati.

"What is Sukhavati?" Vanna asked with a slight inclination of her head.

Sukhavati is the western pure land of the Buddha Amitabha. Sukhavati translates to mean, "Land of

Bliss" In other cultures it is called the Elysium Fields. In Christianity, it is called Heaven.

The only way for Lin Xin to assure that he would continue to live on earth was to keep Nagarjuna in Sukhavati. He does this by keeping Nagarjuna's head and body separated. So He continues what Kumara started by hiding them in different locations.

In other words," Daniel said, shifting in his chair, once the head is reunited with the body, Nagarjuna will walk again here on earth and Lin Xin will be bound to hell for eternity.

"But until then, Nagarjuna is still in Sukhavati and Lin Xin is free to roam earth. Instead of needing blood to live, he must remain on earth collecting the wayward souls of the Sukhavati. Legend states that, mysteriously, every year Nagarjuna's head moves closer to his body and Lin Xin can't do anything to stop it."

"So, for some morbid reason," Vanna interjected, waving her hand in a final flourish, "a corrupt murderer is bound to collect lost souls for heaven in order to stay on earth. Doesn't make any sense, does it?"

Leaning forward, she planked her elbows on the table and cupped her hands under her chin. "Is that what all those papers are about in your desk? The box with the Chinese writing along with your notes? You know I can read Chinese but I couldn't make sense out of any of it. How do you know all this stuff?"

Daniel studied her face to see how much she knew before continuing.

"I have always been interested in eastern mythology. Even as a kid, I was fascinated with the culture, the legends, not to mention the dragons. As a teenager, it was Bruce Lee and martial arts. Throughout my life, I have had this thing about it. I can't explain it, but it's there.

It wasn't until I had bought a collection of relics and antiques from an estate sale before opening the shop that I got back into it. In the collection, there was a small box of old Chinese scrolls. My interest was immediately renewed and I felt drawn to discover the meaning of the scrolls. I went out and picked up everything I could get my hands on to learn more about the scrolls."

Vanna looked puzzled, asking Daniel, "What does that have to do with Lin Xin?"

"Okay, I know this guy, Lin Xin is nuts, but the stuff he knows is beyond anything I have ever read or heard about. When he started coming into the shop right after I opened, he saw the scrolls and books on Lao Tzu and Nagarjuna's works on my desk and that's how the conversation about their meaning started. He is the one that helped me translate Nagarjuna's Tree of Wisdom into English.

It doesn't matter what or how he claims to know this stuff, but he's been like a Rosetta Stone for me in my research."

"How did you figure out who he was? Vanna asked, her eyes transfixed on him. "I want more facts."

"Well," Daniel said, sawing his index fingers across his lower lip, "I didn't put two and two together until I saw him again this morning. But it actually started at your grave, the day of the funeral. After everyone left and the sun was beginning to set, he came up to me and said something strange to me. *'You need to make a decision. The time is near, and it's imperative that you make the right choice.'*

"I had no idea what he was talking about, until I saw him again-morning, when I went to the front yard to see if you were on your way back. He was standing by the gate."

"What did he tell you?" Vanna asked.

Daniel sat back with a poker face, his lips pursed. "He said, "The time is near. Remember that snow always melts at some point. The decision you make will not only dictate your own fate, but Vanna's as well, not only on this earth but in the hereafter."

"What decision?" Vanna's question hung in the air.

"I don't know," Daniel said, shaking his head. "I just don't know. I guess I'll know when the time comes. I imagine it involves both of us. I guess I'm supposed to just step aside and let him do his job, let him take you away."

Vanna and Daniel sat in silence, looking at one another. Daniel took a deep breath and lean over the table and talked, "Remember I said I have been seeing reflections too? When I said it was somebody else, I meant it was Lin Xin. I didn't tell you at the time because I needed to understand for myself."

He suddenly stiffened his body. "But our friend has a big surprise in store for him!" He slapped his hand down hard on the table. You ain't going anywhere unless it's with me, understood?" Daniel gave a conspiratorial smile, stood and began clearing the table.

While cleaning up the dishes, Vanna listened while Daniel tried his best to explain the esoteric nature of Chinese mysticism and mythology. There were other worlds besides this one and with the right key souls could travel between them, that the same stories were in all mystic traditions. Daniel revealed that he had been searching for that key, the key to the other realms. Had Daniel found it? Had he gone to the other realms in search for her after her death?

Conflicting emotions enveloped her. On one hand, she felt safe and secured in Daniel's confidence and calm behavior. On the other, she felt terrified that all of this could end. She felt that Daniel knew more than he was admitting to. A long exhale wisped from her mouth. All she could do was put her faith in him and let be whatever came.

Vanna dropped into the chair still deep in thought.

"Vanna," he said in his nonchalant manner, turning away from the sink, "How much do you remember about the time between your death and coming back?"

She thought about it for a few moments. She struggled to piece together the fragmented impressions and her words came slowly.

"You know, it's so surreal that it's more like a dream" She shook her head. "I know I felt loved and like I had come 'home.' The people, the places, I don't remember. But the feelings and the emotions...I remember them."

"Can you recall how long it seemed that you were there?" He stared intently at her.

"No, other than I searched high and low for you. I remember asking everyone I saw where you were. I seemed to know that I was where I belonged, but something was missing and I can only say that thing was you. I never felt threatened nor was I told I couldn't leave, all I felt was love. Why do you ask?"

"Nothing in particular...other than for you to know that no matter how this plays out, you'll be fine and we'll be together. The one thing I *do* need for you to do is to trust me. I need you to know that *whatever* happens, no matter what, just keep faith that everything will work out."

"But baby, you already know I do. I trust you completely. I know that we will always be together. Don't worry, okay?"

"Okay. Now, go wash up and get ready, we have a date at the park today."

Vanna ambled down the hallway to the bedroom, surprised at Daniel's composure. He acted as if none of this was happening, like he somehow had it all handled. She loved him and had faith in him; she knew no harm would ever come to her as long as they were together. She found it amusing, his asking her to trust him. She had always trusted him, from the very beginning, as if her soul had recognized from the start its counterpart. How could he ask her to trust him? Silly fool, didn't he realize that they were one soul? But it made her feel good. Her comfort came from his strength; he was her rock, her protector.

She thought about how eerily familiar this monstrous apparition was. There was something about Lin Xin that she just couldn't place. Not wanting to worry Daniel any further, she decided to dismiss it as she entered the room.

* * *

Since Vanna's return after her death, Daniel had poured over every scrap of information he could find that would help him understand what was happening. It was a blessing he had spent so many years researching Eastern philosophy. It gave him a much needed head start. Though he hadn't mentioned it, it wasn't as if he were hiding anything from her. He just needed to get his head around it before he could explain it. Above all, he needed to be able to control the situation. But he now faced a new problem. There wasn't enough time.

The day of reckoning was fast approaching. Ready or not, he would have to deal with it best he could. He wiped his sweaty palms on his pants, took a quick breath, crimping his mouth in determination. One way or another, they would be together...either here or somewhere else.

* * *

The day started off sunny but clouds were steadily building to the north. At this time of year in Texas, the weather could change on a dime. However, neither Daniel or Vanna realized the changing weather was a sorrowful harbinger of impending danger to come.

"I'm not going to let the threat of Lin Xin or a little bad weather ruin our day." Daniel called to Vanna as the last of the dishes were washed and put away. He began loading the truck for their date with sandwiches he had made along with some treats, storing them in a box next to the ice chest that was filled with bottled water and fresh iced tea.

Darting back into the house, he snatched up a blanket from the bedroom and on the way out stopped at the hall closet and grabbed his 12 gauge shotgun and pistol. No matter what may come, he was prepared for the worse. By the time the truck was loaded, he turned at the sound of Vanna coming out. Wearing a pink t-shirt and jean shorts he marveled again at her natural beauty. It never failed to take his breath away. The sight of her always squeezed his heart as if every last drop of love was being wrung from it. He knew that his love for her was complete. He was ready for whatever might happen today.

On their way to the park, Vanna leaned forward to turn on the radio to find something she liked. Finding one that matched her mood, she moved closer to Daniel, took his arm and laid her head on his shoulder. Daniel drove with a contented smile. At that moment, it was easy to believe that nothing had ever happened and all was right with the world.

Pulling into the parking lot, he was surprised to see that no one else was there. Sure, there was rain in the forecast but nothing to stop people from being outside.

"Where do you think we should set up." Daniel asked.

"How about under the pavilion just in case it rains?" she said.

Daniel smiled at her choice. He knew she loved being outside in the rain. They walked together carrying the ice chest between them with the box of goodies he had prepared that morning resting on top. She began setting up while he went back to the truck to get the rest of the stuff. Out of the corner of his eye, he caught a glimpse of Lin Xin, standing at the edge of the woods. Daniel kept walking, not wanting to let on that he saw him. Daniel had plans for him. At the truck, he slyly tucked the pistol into the waistband of his jeans and wrapped the shotgun in the blanket.

Returning to the pavilion, he noticed that Lin Xin had somehow managed to beat him there. Vanna stood confronting him by the table. He hustled forward to block Vanna, his eyes never leaving Lin Xin.

"Step aside, Vanna!" She quickly moved, putting the table between her and Lin Xin, her face expressing a surprising calm. Daniel had to believe that it was his cool and methodical behavior. For that, he was glad. He only hoped it would last.

Daniel, with a nod, acknowledged his presence, "Lin Xin."

Lin Xin stood there, grinning, "To whom are you trying to prove something, Daniel? To me? To her? My dear friend, you are nothing more than a pitiful, pathetic insect. Go on, admit it … tell her that you can't save her. You are just as helpless now as you were on the day she died. You failed her then and you're going to fail her today." He shifted his focus to Vanna,

"And you. Yes, you, Vanna. Are you so blind that you believe this man can save you? My dear niece, you are such a fool. You are both fools! While your belief in him is sweet, it's childish. He can't stop me. You both need to wake up! You're living a lie and it will damn you both to hell! There are consequences for your defiance and contemptuous behavior and *I am* those consequences."

Daniel wasn't to be easily intimidated. He wasn't backing down now, when his entire life and any chance for happiness were at stake. "Vanna is staying here with me, Lin Xin. You're not taking her anywhere."

"Neither of you," he said, condescendingly, his mouth framing a twisted smile, "are thoroughly acquainted with the evil standing before you. You cannot begin to imagine what is in store for you. Your cleverness only demonstrates your stupidity. Daniel, I have exhausted my patience with you. Step aside, let me take what is rightfully mine and I'll let you live. You are a defeated man and behind every defeated man is a frustrated love. Accept your fate and go."

Daniel laughed turned and looked at Vanna, "I forgot to tell you, this guy loves to hear himself talk."

Returning his attention to Lin Xin, Daniel said, "Really? Call me an insect? Is that all you've got? Geez, Lin Xin, you really need to learn how to insult someone. Now, let me tell you what I think. He pulled his eyebrows together until they scrunched together on the bridge of his nose.

"Your *arrogance* will be your downfall." He pointed an accusatory finger at him. "It took me awhile to figure it out but you fucked up when you spoke to me at the funeral. If you had any power, you wouldn't need to play big shot now and try to scare us. If you are what you say, then you would have taken Vanna the first day she came back. But you didn't, and that was the puzzle I have been working on. In your arrogance I found the answer... You need us to believe in you to have any power over us. We don't. You have no power and you can't tear us apart. You are nothing more than a puppet with someone else pulling the strings!"

Lin Xin's face flushed an ugly red. Clenching his fists, he shouted, "I am not a puppet!" He took an aggressive step forward and roared, "I am a King!"

"No," Daniel said, shaking his head back and forth and then fixing Lenox with an unflinching stare. "You're nothing but a piece of shit." Daniel reached for the blanket-covered shot gun and yanked the cover off.

At the sight of the shotgun, Lin Xin began to laugh like a maniac, "You can't kill me! You cannot stop me!"

Daniel knew inwardly that he couldn't kill him, but that wasn't the plan. He had another agenda in mind. "I know that, asshole, but this is for fucking with my wife. No one fucks with her, especially you."

Daniel, now out of words, unloaded every round of the shotgun into Lennox's gut. Vanna watched in horror as every shot hit its mark with deadly intent. Flesh torn and blood-spattered, or what looked like blood, Lennox stood there laughing, taking everything Daniel had to give him.

Lin Xin looked down at the carnage and said, "Is that all you got, Cowboy?"

With the shotgun emptied, Daniel dropped it to the ground and pulled out his pistol, a cold, black Smith and Wesson Model '59 that held 15 rounds. He became the Smith & Wesson, cold, calculated. It was the only means to bring this madness to an end.

"Not quite," said Daniel, his lips curling with revulsion at Lin Xin's hideous smirk. Holding the gun at eye level he emptied the weapon point blank into his head. He wanted to wipe that arrogant grin off of Lin Xin's face even if it meant taking his face with it. With half the clip spent, Lin Xin began to waver, his body rocking with each shot, until the last shot felled him and he lay sprawled on the ground. Amazing how fifteen rounds was more than enough to shut the guy up. Some demon, Daniel thought.

Daniel stood still for a moment, letting his victory over Lin Xin sink in, then took the few steps to his body, stood over him legs straddled, and said, "Now what, motherfucker?"

The way Daniel said that, coupled with the deadly expression on his face, couldn't keep Vanna from letting let out a nervous laugh.

Her laugh caught Daniel's attention. In one look, he could see the relief in her eyes, even though she was still shaking uncontrollably. Returning his Smith and Wesson to the waistband of his jeans, he picked up the shotgun without a word, wrapped his arm around Vanna and led her up the knoll to the truck.

 But they only made it half way.

The sky suddenly plunged into darkness. The winds increased and the temperature dropped drastically bringing a bone-penetrating chill. The wail of sirens filled the air, warning of the impending danger of the approaching storm.

A crushing pain like a steel vise hit into Daniel's right shoulder. Then he felt as if a hole had been blown through his chest. "Not so fast," was all he heard before falling to his knees. He began to lose consciousness, but before he did, he looked up and saw the terror in Vanna's face. He tried to speak to her, to tell her that everything would be alright, that he had a plan, but no words came out.

Insidious laughter filled his ears and in the distance he heard Lin Xin's voice "This is going to be fun."

His head snapped back with a loud crack and he fell to the ground, his head twisted at an unnatural angle. Sheer terror filled him, aware of his impending death, something he never imagined he would experience.

His vision began to fade, but he could see Vanna being dragged away, kicking and screaming. Knowing from the get-go that this had been a one-way trip with no return passage he repeated in his heart over and over, "It's almost over, baby, it's almost over."

Fat drops of cold rain pelted his body as he slipped into a claustrophobic darkness pierced only by the sounds of angst in Vanna's voice.

"Vanna," he gasped, "it will always be you that I love. Maybe in death we'll be together … together in the Elysium Fields."

<u>The Interview - Conclusion</u>

"That was a hell of a story, Robert. Talk about an ending!"

"Yep, the epic spectacular ... failure."

"So, what happened to them? Vincent's eyes widened. "I mean, did they finally get to be together in the afterlife, in the Elysium Fields?"

"Now, Vinny, not all stories end with happily ever after."

"I know but there's just the one thing - I loved it, don't get me wrong, but why did you tell me? That wasn't exactly what I had imagined for an interview."

"Everything you need to know is in that story. Look at it as a confessional of sorts. The funny thing about fiction is it's nothing more than non-fiction disguised as fiction. There's nothing new under the sun. It's all the same, just told in different ways."

The old man was speaking in riddles, not making any sense at all. While he wanted to hear the end to the story, he had to think of his assignment, although trying to ask Robert a direct question never quite brought the results he wanted.

"I still have a list of questions for you, Robert. Do you mind if we get back to-?"

"Like I said," Robert interrupted, "all the answers you are looking for are in that story. Besides, I'm getting tired. Why don't we call it a day?"

One thing Vincent knew for sure was not to push Robert any further, not out of fear of a shotgun escort but out of professional courtesy. Plus, you never knew if the old man would have a change of heart and call the interview off.

Robert stood and stretched, then ambled over to the stove with Vincent's cup to refill it.

"You're not going to have another cup of tea with me, Robert?"

"Nah, I'm fine," he said, shuffling to the front door and studying the landscape visible through the half pane of glass.

Vincent took that moment of silence to think about the story and what it all meant. Setting his cup down, he focused in on the initials carved on the corner of the table, eyeing them once again - *'dva4ever'*. Studying, he thought about the flooring...heart of pine. No, it can't be, he's playing with me. He also eyed the third cup that still sat on the table before an empty chair. And what's up with that? he wondered. He didn't remember Robert placing it in front of the other chair. The more he thought about it, the more he concluded that Robert was a master at playing with his mind. He clamped his mouth into a thin line, angry at the thought that the entire afternoon was nothing more than an old man's attempt at screwing with him by making up a crazy story, 'I have a tale to tell', he mimicked. What a load of horse shit.

Robert broke the quiet, "The sun goes down fast this time of year. You might want to consider getting out of the high country before it gets too dark since you don't know your way around."

The abrupt hint to leave bewildered Vincent making him all the more agitated. Without a word, he downed the rest of his tea in one, scalding gulp, got up from the table and shoved his notes into his bag and headed for the door, trying to maintain a degree of professionalism by stopping long enough to shake Robert's hand and thank him for the interview. Moving across the porch and down the steps, he trudged with meaningful steps toward his car. He couldn't wait to get back to the city. He looked back at the porch to wave goodbye and all he could see was a smirk on the old man's face that said, "Gotcha, Sonny."

Vincent wished he could tell the old man to fuck off but, instead, mutterer under his breath, "Of all the twisted, convoluted, bullshit stories. Fucking asshole. What a con man. He thought of the character in *The Usual Suspects*. The only thing missing in this scenario was Verbal Kint.

So consumed with anger, especially with the fact that his career was basically over with, he didn't notice an old Asian man walking up the drive and nearly ran him over. He thought back on Robert's story. "Jet Li, my ass. Nagarjuna? Lao Tzu? You nutty old bastard. Fuck you!" He turned onto the main road and headed back to Colorado Springs.

* * *

Standing on the porch, keeping an eye on the driveway as the old Asian man made his way up to the cabin, Robert said, "How about one last cup of tea before we go?"

Feeling the warm touch of a soft hand on his back, he heard, "Sure, baby, I'll heat the water for us."

"Make enough for three. Nagarjuna's coming."

Robert smiled at a life lived well, proud of what he had accomplished, especially the opportunity to tell his story. His own death was the only way he managed to foil Lin Xin's plan by bringing Nagarjuna's head and body back together which sent Lin Xin to Hell forever.

Turning, he saw his whole reason for being standing at the stove, dressed in a black silk dress wearing a silver charm bracelet...a woman so beautiful, she reminded him of a Zhou Princess.

Other Books by Dennis Waller

The Tao Te Ching, A Translation by Dennis Waller

The Hsin Hsin Ming by Dennis Waller

Nagarjuna's Tree of Wisdom, A Translation by Dennis Waller

The Tao of Kenny Loggins by Dennis Waller

The Way of the Tao, Living an Authentic Life by Dennis Waller

The Art of Talking to Christ by Dennis Waller

Indigo Wisdom by Francesca Rivera and Dennis Waller

Are You an Indigo? Discover Your Authentic Self by Dennis Waller

9 Keys You Must Master to be a Miserable Asshole

9 Things You Must Know Before Starting a Business

Zen and Tao, A Little Book on Buddhist Thought and Meditation

The Importance of the Tao, A Short Essay

Texas Jack's Famous Pralines Secret Recipe Book

For an exclusive sneak peek into the continuing sage of this tale, send an email to Dennis Waller at "dennismwaller@yahoo.com" You'll receive an inside look at the next installment before its official release.

ABOUT THE AUTHOR

Dennis Waller, author of several books, is recognized as an expert on spiritual experience, self-discovery, and exploring the human consciousness. As writer, speaker and philosopher, his teachings invoke an introspective view on how to discover one's true authentic self through a higher sense of consciousness and awareness. He teaches classes in the Dallas area on several subjects including Enochian Magic and Developing Your Psychic Abilities. He is best known for his work in the field of Indigos, people who possess unusual or supernatural abilities.

His other fields of expertise include comparative religion, the law of attraction, and interpreting Eastern thought's relevancy to science and quantum physics. He is in demand as a guest speaker on radio programs, a lecturer at churches and life enrichment groups, and conducts workshops for Indigos.

He doesn't like long walks on the beach at night nor does he care for round balloons but does enjoy an occasional butterfly or cricket on a stick but only if served with fries. This bit of non-sense is included to see if you really read these bios. If you have then you will enjoy his sense of humor. Never take life too seriously, you will die someday so make the most of it, go out for an ice-cream, feed the ducks and tell someone you love that you do love them, even if you're mad at them, unless you're really mad like someone I know, then, maybe a phone call would be better.

Now, enough with the non-sense, but really, find a way to enjoy live and love!

PS- feel free to contact Dennis at

dennismwaller@yahoo.com

7394573R00069

Printed in Great Britain
by Amazon.co.uk, Ltd.,
Marston Gate.